TAKE ME

CRIMSON PACK TRILOGY

A. LONERGAN

NIGHT SHADE PRESS, LLC

*This book is dedicated to **me**. It's dedicated to the girl I once was. The girl that loved bad boys and paid heavily for it over and over again. This book is dedicated to the broken me. The imperfect me. The me that needed to be loved in a very toxic world. <u>Allyssa, you worked so hard to get to this place. Never forget that you deserve it all.</u>*

CHAPTER 1
JADE RIVERS

The music thumping through the speakers did something to my insides. Every single party. Every single time. It made me feel a way I could never feel when I was at home, especially when I was alone. I closed my eyes and my body moved with the music. Every beat drop, every thrum, every note. I sighed with contentment. My body stayed with the tempo. Music was the only thing that could break me from my shy shell. It was the only thing that gave me the nerve to approach guys, especially the ones with the tattoos and piercings. It was the one thing in my lonely life that gave me something my parents couldn't buy. It made me feel.

Tonight there was someone new. There was always someone new, but this one didn't look like the bad boy type. No, this one didn't pretend to be bad. His arms were covered which was a surprise for how hot it got in these parties. His face was clear from any piercings and his hair was cropped short. No, he didn't look like the typical bad boy I went for. But he didn't need to *look* dangerous, he felt it. Danger rolled off of him in giant waves, waves bigger than the music pulsing from the speakers. He held a beer in his hand but he didn't take a sip from it. He watched the room with calculating eyes. Eyes that seemed cold when they finally landed on me. But cold was the last thing that I felt with his gaze washing over my body.

If it hadn't been for the music wrapping around me, I wouldn't have grinned at him. My lips stretched away from my teeth and I gave him the best smile I could muster. His dark brow inched up his forehead and he turned away from me. I ran my tongue over the front of my teeth as the smile disappeared. He wasn't here to pick up women, he was here for something else. Something I couldn't give him. Which was fine because there was a man at the other side of the room giving me the grin I had just tucked away. This one had a gold ring through his lip and his neck was covered in black, swirling tattoos. My heart skittered to a stop. I winked at him and closed my eyes as I continued to move to the music. Maybe he would get the hint, maybe not. Whether or not he did, it didn't matter. I would carry on with my night and someone else would try to entertain me.

After a few seconds, the right amount of time it would have taken for him to get to me, I opened my eyes. I was ready to throw him a disappointed pout, except he was gone. And so was Mr. Danger that had been hanging out on the other side of the room with his untouched beer.

My Apple Watch dinged on my wrist and I groaned. I knew this was going to happen. I had wasted too much time scoping the guys out and not enough time making moves.

A text rolled through from my Dad- *"Your car isn't in the driveway. Don't forget you still have a curfew while we are away."*

I pushed through the throngs of people bumping and grinding against each other. The front door was wide open and the lawn to this home was trashed with beer bottles and red plastic cups. I stepped over a passed out couple on the front steps. The cold metal of my car keys dug between my thumb and my pointer finger. I knew better than to walk to my car alone this late at night and not be prepared to fight. It had happened a few times. I liked to party alone and it had caused some of the worst types to take notice. Not in the ways I liked either.

The ones that followed you to your car in the middle of the night weren't looking for something kinky, more like something permanent. Like death. My keys had saved my life more times than I wanted to count. You would have thought I would have come to learn not to go to parties alone anymore, but I kept coming back. Any rager was a good time, even if it meant a little danger in the process. After all, that thrill did pull me in.

But that was my problem, I had always been attracted to the bad boys. The bullies especially. The ones that had such a bad, wicked gleam in their eye that most people had the right mind to stay away. Not me. There was something about that sinful gleam that had me coming back for more each time.

This time had been a bust though. My parents had surveillance all around the house. They loved to know what their only child was doing while they went away on vacation. I didn't mind, I preferred the solitude, but I didn't exactly like the constant watch in the sky. When I did get to go on vacation with them, when I wasn't at school, it was always enjoyable. In fact, I probably got into more trouble while we weren't in our little university town. Parties were always better internationally.

The wet grass squashed under my boots as I found my car one street away from the party. The party I didn't remember getting an invite to. I scratched my neck as I thought about it. How had I even learned about this party? It wasn't like it was a secret but usually I could remember more about it like a text or a flyer that had been passed around after class or stapled to a door somewhere.

The music could still be heard from all the way over here, even after I got into my car and closed the door. I was surprised the police hadn't been called yet.

My little beater car started up quietly and I pulled away from the street that was entirely too close to the university I attended. That was probably why the cops hadn't been dispatched. There weren't many people around here who cared, who weren't at the party themselves, and the rest? They were probably too old to hear the music anyway.

When I pulled into my freshly pressure-washed driveway another text rolled through on my watch.

Mom- *"Thanks for meeting curfew! Goodnight, I love you!"*

I narrowed my eyes at the doorbell camera. It

was creepy that they knew everything. But they had grown up in a time that didn't have all of this. They reminded me daily of the kind of peace it gave them to be able to see anything and everything on their property. One of these days I was going to figure out how to put it on a loop.

CHAPTER 2
JADE RIVERS

Fire was all everyone could talk about come Monday. The party I had attended had turned more than rowdy after I had left. The upstairs bedroom had been ablaze while the rest of the house was untouched by it. The rumors swirled around me as I tried to pay attention in my classes and walk around on campus. No matter where I turned, everyone had something to say about what happened. No one knew anything according to the police. There were plenty of things that didn't add up about it either, starting with the room being completely incinerated but the remnants of blood sprayed across the walls. How could they tell that if the room had burned so hot that they couldn't identify bodies? The bodies had been burned so badly that all they could do was guess on who they were and go by eyewitness accounts. Neck tattoo boy had been one of the ones to go into the bedroom and never come out. At least that's what the whispers said.

There didn't look to be foul play but there wasn't much to go off of. The police around campus knew a few students were into blood and fire play, and without a body, what could they prove?

I buried my hands in my hair as my history professor droned on about Ancient Egypt. It was usually my favorite topic but I couldn't stop thinking about the guy from the party. If I had escaped with him that night, would he still have died or would we both be dead? A chill washed down my spine and I rubbed my hands down my arms to keep myself warm. I wasn't usually cold in class, but something wasn't right about what had happened at the party. Would this put a snag on others in the future? I felt guilty for even wondering that. But a girl had to get out and have a good time somehow. My professor cut his lecture short and laughed. It startled me from my thoughts.

"I always get so passionate about this!" He plucked his wire-frame glasses from his nose. "Your essays will be due next Monday. No class on Wednesday! Have a great week."

I doubted I would be able to focus on any of it, my brain felt fried, which was weird enough. Usually after a good party, I felt rejuvinated and ready to crush all of my classes. I knew saving it for the weekend was a bust too. There was another party but this one was at one of the frat houses. An excited thrill washed through me as I read the text on my watch.

My friend Tracey from my math class texted me to tell me about it. I didn't know if she was really a friend or just a fellow partier. But I didn't mind. I enjoyed being let in on all of the school drama as well as the free booze that would come with the weekend. I didn't always drink, but if Tracey was going to be there, I could let loose. I trusted her in a way I didn't let myself trust others. I usually stayed away from others, but somehow she had managed to wiggle her way into my heart and life.

The rest of the week passed in a blur. I finished my essay at the library on Wednesday and forced myself to stop listening to the drama around campus about neck tat dude. It was bad enough he had been killed, but now no one would stop talking about it. His favored parking spot was full of flowers and art. After the first time I had walked past it, I decided I could park on the other side of campus. There was something about death that didn't feel good. The thought of it always made me want to panic. With it being so close to me, I didn't like it even more. It could have been me up there. How would my parents handle that?

Loss had never been something I had to go through, but I had seen enough movies to get the gist. Just one more day to the party and I could forget everything. I could get lost in the music again and hopefully find some hot company for the rest of the night. But it also meant that my nights would be cut short because my parents were coming home Sunday. That wasn't something I wanted to think about either. That meant until their next vacation all they would want to do was stay up my butt. No late nights, no parties, and especially no boys. I missed them, but I liked having my freedom. I loved being able to go and do as I pleased with them only worrying about my curfew.

Thank goodness Tracey was going to be there and I could finally let it all go. I could finally party to my heart's content. My last night of freedom for a little while. I could wait one more night.

I turned this way and that in the mirror. My hair was pulled up and away from my face. My clothes were as tight as I could manage. Tonight was going to be the night, the night I completely let go. It was time. I was going to find the guy that had danger coming off of him in tidal waves and I was going to kiss him. I was going to enjoy every single moment of this night. I was going to do what I could to seduce him. I deserved it, after all. It was like a treat for myself. I had finished my essay, I was making good grades, why couldn't I just let it all go for one night? What could go wrong?

I took a sip from my silver flask. The whiskey burned all the way down but I loved the feeling. Just a few more minutes and Tracey would be here. My parents wouldn't have a clue I was out and I would get to stay out all night. Possibly even until the morning if Mr. Danger was there tonight. I was counting on it. He was the prize that I would do anything to obtain. I tucked a pack of gum into my over the shoulder bag, an extra pair of panties, and my travel contact solution with the case. I was usually more careful than this. I didn't go home with strangers. I didn't drink when I actually got to the party and I always drove.

Tonight I was tossing caution to the wind. I was going to cut loose in every single way possible. I only had, maybe, one more year in this little college town. Graduation was right around the corner. I could practically taste it. I ran my hands down the front of my black leather skirt and readjusted the laces on my knee-high boots. My off the shoulder crop top clung to me like a second skin as I rushed down the stairs. The doorbell rang and I tugged at the hem on the shirt for a moment. This was the most risqué thing I had worn. I knew my parents would see me leaving and coming home. I couldn't risk my parents actually knowing what I was doing. We had to be extra careful.

Tracey held up her backpack and spilled out her favorite lie. Just in case my parents listened over the doorbell camera like I knew they would. "You ready to study?"

She wore gray sweatpants with an oversized sweater. I didn't know how she wasn't sweating herself to death in the getup. But I also knew she was going to strip as soon as she was in the den. I kicked the door closed and smirked. The sweater came off first then she shucked the pants.

Under the pants were skintight black pleather leggings. A leopard tank top was tucked into them. She pulled her ponytail holder from her hair and light honey curls bounced around her shoulders. She shoved her clothes into her backpack.

"Where did you park?" I checked my reflecion in the mirror that was hanging in the hallway by the kitchen.

"Two streets over, just in case." She winked as she put massive gold hoops in her ears. Her tan skin glistened like she had sprayed herself with a glitter mist. But I knew better, she always looked like a goddess. I envied her beautiful skin tone.

She smiled and the little gap between her front teeth flashed. "I can't believe we have to do this to keep your parents off of your trail."

I rolled my eyes. "Not everyone can be as lucky as you. You get to live in the dorms while my parents moved our entire home to the campus town and they're hardly here to enjoy this massive home."

She grimaced. "True, let's get going," She took a long sniff. "You pregaming without me?"

I tossed her the silver flask as we stomped up the stairs. It wouldn't be easy to sneak out but I was determined. My parents had thought they didn't need cameras on my side of the house because my window was practically impossible to get to. They *loved* to underestimate me. The locks clicked as I flicked them away from the window. The glass groaned as I shoved upward with all of my strength. It had been a few months since I had opened it and it was in desperate need of some oil, but there was no way I was going to tell my father that. I would have to dig in the garage for it later. I had a feeling this was going to be a regular thing. Keeping a can of WD-40 under the bed would hardly be my worst sin.

The eave of the house was at least four feet from my window and then from there, it was another five-foot drop. The only problem was that the eave was at an angle. I had to kick off just right or I would completely miss it and fall the nine feet. I had done this a few times for practice. Just in case this moment arose, but that didn't mean that my feet weren't sweating just thinking about what was about to happen. I rolled my shoulders and relaxed my limbs before I swung my legs outside of the window and perched there.

If I didn't get this right it could be very bad. I flexed my fingers on the window sill. Tracey grabbed my arm. "What? We are jumping to that?"

I nodded my head and shook her hand off. I had told her this wouldn't be easy but she had insisted. I could have stayed in another night but she wanted to get me drunk too badly to wait a few weeks for my parents to leave again. I didn't mind this. Adrenaline was the sweet drug coursing through my veins right now. I liked the feeling.

As I shoved away from the side of the house, I felt like I could fly. For a brief moment it felt good, then my feet hit the shingles and I started to slide a little bit. Little pebbles dug into my palms and I was glad I had pulled my hair up and away from my face. Sweat slid down my temples. I prayed it didn't smudge my makeup.

Tracey looked down at me with her wide topaz eyes. "I don't think I can do this."

My feet slid on the roof as I scooted down the shingles. I would have to get to the ground before she jumped. I couldn't risk her missing the roof. I would have to try to catch her if something went wrong. I gripped the gutters and lowered my body down from the perch. It wasn't even considered a roof, more like a decorative piece of shingles that made the house look like it had dimension. It jutted out from the side of the house in an odd way and didn't really do much but keep the water from splashing up on the dining room window. My body hung there for a few seconds before I dropped to the ground into a crouch. My knees gave out in the process and I sprawled onto the grass. I heaved a breath and shoved myself up from the ground. That wasn't so bad.

Tracey shook her head. "What about the window?"

"Pull it down a little."

Surprise rang through me as she managed to pull it down enough so only her butt was inside. Her chest rose and fell rapidly as she pushed off of the side of the house and sailed through the air. Her arms windmilled around wildly and a soft shriek escaped her lips as her feet barely made it to the edge of the roof. Her hands scrambled for something to grip as her body slid down the shingles.

"No, no, no," she gasped as her body left the side of the house and she tumbled down. I rushed to get under her and soften her fall. The impact of her body was a lot more than I had expected. It knocked the breath from my chest as we both hit the soft grass.

Tracey rolled off of me and ran her hands over her body like she couldn't believe she was still alive. The roof had softened the fall some. If she hadn't made it to the roof, this would have all been much worse. I sat up and unscrewed the flask that I had retrieved from my bag. I dumped the rest of the contents in my mouth and scrunched my nose as I swallowed the fire down. At least her body hadn't killed me. That would have been a story to tell.

The buzz was starting to work its way through my limbs and I could feel myself getting more fluid. It wouldn't take me long at all to get completely wasted tonight, but that was only if Mr. Danger wasn't there.

CHAPTER 3
JADE RIVERS

The house we had bought just a few short years ago butted up to the woods that circled the little university town. It had creeped me out the first two years of college. Especially when my parents had started to go on vacation. It had started with an anniversary trip and then a birthday trip which eventually led to more trips throughout the year. Mom had felt guilty after the first year of them being gone but then Dad had reassured her that parents didn't usually hover like they did. Parents were supposed to enjoy their lives, especially when their children went off to college and they worked remotely.

But three rounds of in-vitro fertilization and seven years of infertility would do that to a couple. I didn't mind that they had always hovered, but after I had turned eighteen it had started to get slightly annoying. Even when Dad wasn't very convincing that their vacationing was valid, I chimed in and helped. I loved the freedom and the massive house they left behind. But the freedom had been short-lived when a door to door salesman had sold the whole package of surveillance with a shiny red bow. They didn't need much convincing to leave after that. I was happy to see them go too. They had given up so much to have me and then to raise me. I didn't mind them leaving to do whatever it was that they wanted now.

As much as the woods scared me, it was the only way we could get out of the yard without being spotted by the motion detector cameras posted almost all the way around the house. If we hugged the fence, they wouldn't see us. Which was good because the last thing I wanted to do was hop the fence and come face to face with the mean-ass dog next door. We hopped the back fence easily.

The mean-ass dog next door took that moment to bark at us and I could have sworn my soul left my body in shock. I clutched my chest as we ran for the cover of the trees. My body was on high alert but the adrenaline hadn't worn off yet plus there was a whole lot of whiskey in my system. I grinned at Tracey as she shined her phone flashlight into the woods. All we had to do was go a few feet and we would be out.

An eery howl split the air and Tracey wrapped her arms around my middle. We both stayed locked in that embrace for a few seconds before we rushed the rest of the way out of the forest. We didn't bother with looking back because as soon as we broke the line of the woods the howl rang out again. We took off into a run. The street light was the only bit of hope we had as we raced away from the shadows of the woods. We slid to a stop on the pavement and I gripped Tracey's hand in mine as we both bent over at the waist and laughed. It sounded slightly hysterical but what did it matter? Somehow we had managed to live through the entire ordeal. First the crazy escape from the house and now wild animals. What could possibly happen next?

The buzz I had developed was long gone, the adrenaline had shoved all the alcohol out of my system. The hair on the back of my neck pebbled as we walked. I couldn't shake the feeling that we were either being watched or followed. Every few seconds I looked over my shoulder. Her black SUV waited for us at the end of the third street and I could have sworn we both picked up our pace to get inside of it. We leaned our heads against the seat and locked the doors as soon as we got in. I could hardly breathe and judging by how rapid Tracey's chest was rising and falling, she was struggling too.

"I'm going to need a few drinks to get this out of my system," Tracey started her car and pulled away from the curb. But even as we drove down the road, I couldn't shake the feeling that something was still watching us. I clenched my hands together and shook my head. I felt silly and I wondered if paranoia was hereditary.

The streetlights vibrated the closer we got to the frat house. Chills washed over my arms and down my spine. It probably wasn't normal for me to get this excited about a party, but I couldn't help myself. It was my guilty pleasure after all. Tracey parked close to the house and kicked the car door open. I was a little more graceful with my movements, I was wearing a tight leather skirt. My small bag thumped against my back as I walked to the frat house.

Tracey grabbed my hand to pull me to a stop.

She held up her hand that had her watch on it. "You have the walkie talkie app?"

I nodded my head. It was the first thing she had made me download when we had gone out together the first time. I swatted her worried hands away. "Yes, and I know if I need you it's just a click of a button."

"Cut loose tonight and have fun. Don't worry about any silly boys." Her topaz eyes stared holes into mine. "Please be careful, and don't do anything I wouldn't do. Stay away from the dangerous ones tonight."

"Of course!" But honestly, when I had alcohol in my system it made it harder for me to stay away from the bad boys. And Mr. Danger himself had just been on the balcony smoking a cigarette. The sight had put me on cloud nine. I rolled my shoulders and marched forward. Alcohol never seemed to affect Tracey the way it did everyone else, so I never worried about her like she did with me.

I grabbed a White Claw from the tub at the front door and stepped over bodies littered around the foyer. It wasn't even midnight yet and everyone was sloshed already. Leave it to the lightweights to make this party a drag. A few boys from my classes gave me appreciative looks and I completely overlooked them. I wasn't interested in Kyle from Algebra or

Jeremy from Creative Writing. I didn't entertain their advances in class, what would make them think I would entertain them here?

Alcohol. I rolled my eyes and managed to bob out the way of their path. The hairs on the back of my neck stood up and I peered over my shoulder.

There he was.

Mr. Danger stared holes into my back. His golden eyes met mine and there was something familiar there. Tonight there was a bit of stubble on his chin and he wore a button-down flannel shirt. His jeans were ripped at the knees but not in the intentional way that most guys bought. No these jeans looked worn down from hard use and long hours. My stomach clenched. Even his boots were worn. This was more than dangerous.

The corner of his mouth quirked up as he caught me staring like I hadn't caught him just a few seconds before. I forced my eyes back to his and his nostrils flared. He turned away quickly and went right back up the stairs. A hand on my shoulder made me jump but I was ready to swing if it was one of the guys from my classes. No one was going to put their hands on me. I tensed beneath the hand before I swung around. My little handbag bounced against my lower back.

"You okay?" Tracey's voice met my ears.

I tugged on my tight top and popped my White Claw open. I was most certainly not okay. My legs trembled and my heart did this weird skitter in my chest. "Totally, great."

She narrowed her bright eyes at me. "You sure? You look a little pale. Someone here bothering you?"

I took a sip from my drink and winced. It wasn't my cup of tea but I had grabbed the first thing I had seen. I had always preferred the burn of Whiskey but parties like these didn't usually supply the good stuff. I was picky but I also wanted to get drunk. I couldn't be picky at a party like this. But Jello Shots would probably do better. I handed the canned drink to my friend and stumbled through the throngs of people cluttered everywhere. A light shone through the darkness of the living room and I knew immediately that it had to be the kitchen. I grinned to myself as I continued to shove through the gyrating bodies.

Someone shoved my shoulder and I found myself against a wall. I took a deep breath and closed my eyes before I punched the face of the man that had me pinned. My temper would do me no favors here. I opened my eyes and came face to face with Mr. Danger. The skin between my eyebrows pulled together as I looked at him.

He smiled down at me as I narrowed my eyes up at him. "Hey there, you should probably watch where you're going."

I raised my eyebrows at him this time. "Excuse me? You ran into me." I motioned between our bodies up against the wall. He was the one pressed into me. It wasn't the other way around. Though I didn't exactly mind it. He smelled slightly of cigarettes, pine, and whiskey. Cigarettes weren't the best in that mix but somehow, he made it smell heavenly.

His yellow eyes twinkled and they reminded me of Tracey's. He pulled away from me and shrugged before he downed the contents in his drink. I watched as his throat bobbed before he lowered his cup. "Then I guess I owe you an apology."

"I guess you do." I crossed my arms over my chest as my eyebrow raised in a challenge.

"Can I get you a drink?" he asked as he pointed to the kitchen with his empty cup. "Pick your poison and I'll do what I can to make your dream come true."

"Whiskey, neat. No cheap stuff."

He leaned in and pressed his nose to the base of my neck. I stiffened but then his scent wrapped around me again and I began to loosen up. I leaned into his touch but as soon as I made contact he jerked away from me like he had been burned.

He ducked his face away from me and muttered, "I'll see what I can do."

CHAPTER 4

RAFE CRIMSON

A whiskey girl, eh.

She didn't seem like the type. But I did always like them feisty. The way she had turned on me showed me just how much of a fighter she was, which was good because she was going to need it after all this was over.

CHAPTER 5
JADE RIVERS

Mr. Danger came back as promised with a red plastic cup. I couldn't see the contents in it as he got closer and for a moment I felt silly. I knew the dangers that came with these men and sometimes drugging girls came with the territory. I could admit that I liked a true blue bad boy but being drugged wasn't on my 'to do' list. I could go without that one. He didn't smile at me as he got closer. He shoved the cup into my hands and looked me in the eye as he took a sip from his. I eyed his lips as he swallowed down his drink.

He chewed on the inside of his lip. "I'm Rafe,"

"Jade,"

He nodded his head like he already knew then he eyed my drink. "You gonna drink that?"

Nervous butterflies ignited in my stomach. I

didn't make a move to take a sip even though I whispered, "Yes,"

He snatched the cup from my fingers and took a huge gulp from my cup before he put it back in my hand. I couldn't fight the smile that took over my face. I took a sip then and let the alcohol burn through my body.

Any other time, any other party I would have been able to tell you if it was the good stuff but as it slid down my throat Rafe's eyes practically glowed in the dark and the last thing I was worried about was if I was drinking the good stuff. All rational thought flew right out the window and I imagined if he kept it up with his glowing eyes, my panties would be next. I pulled my bottom lip in between my teeth and he moved in toward me again. My heart did that weird skitter again and I wondered if this was the guy that was going to take me home tonight. It was still relatively early but that hadn't stopped me before. His molten liquid eyes flicked to my lips and I knew I was a goner.

My head was a fuzzy mess. Was I lying down? Was I on a bed or had I fallen on the floor? Where was I?

Had I drank that much? The last thing I remembered was one cup of alcohol. I didn't think I had gotten sloshed that quickly. I could hear Tracey's voice filtering through with Rafe's. Something wasn't right. My eyes burned as I tried to roll over. Nothing was making sense in my brain.

"You promised me you would stay away from her," Tracey yelled.

"Everything is different now, you don't understand," Rafe replied back.

"You *promised*," Tracey pleaded.

What were they talking about? Tracey and Rafe knew each other? That didn't make sense. She had seen him on the stairwell, why hadn't she said anything? Or maybe she hadn't seen him after all. Nothing was adding up. My legs felt funny as I tried to move. My eyes felt like they were glued shut.

"All bets are off, I can't have her die."

Tracey scoffed and I finally managed to blink my eyes open. The room was dark. "Die? DIE? I would never let anything happen to her, I promised you that much."

"Do you not listen? Everything is different now, Tracey!"

"Rafe, I'm warning you, walk away." Tracey's voice came out in a growl. I blinked in the darkness.

Growl? Something was seriously messing with my head. This had to be drugs.

"Fine,"

I rolled my shoulders and the room came into view. It wasn't a very quick progression but I was getting mobility back and that was all that mattered. I needed to get away. Fear coursed through me. Adrenaline was gone and had been replaced with panic. With dread. My mouth felt like I had been chewing on a ball of cotton, like after I had my wisdom teeth removed. My stomach dropped as it hit me.

Oh crap, he had drugged me. I rolled over and felt nausea building in my stomach. No, no, no, I couldn't throw up now. I needed to get out. Footsteps sounded on the other side of the room and I zeroed in on the worn boots. I couldn't pretend I was still out of it. I had to go, now. I shoved off of the bed and tilted sideways as I tried to get my bearings. Everything spun around me.

The room was dark but I could still make out the shape of Rafe as he prowled to the bed. I managed to roll away from him but then I saw something shiny clutched in his fist. A syringe. I didn't worry about the fact that I didn't have my purse. I had to go, that was all that mattered.

I had to live and I couldn't live as a junky. That had to be what was in the needle, right? Or were there more dangerous contents in that syringe that could kill me? I had done a lot of things, but nothing like this. I had never been this close to terror. Tears blurred my vision as I scrambled away from him. Tracey must have seen the syringe at the same time. As soon as I was off the bed, she was screaming.

"RUN! Don't look back!"

I wanted to worry about Tracey but for some reason, I knew he didn't care about her. This was all about me. My feet didn't want to work as I stumbled to the door and crashed into it. I wrapped my fingers around the doorknob when I felt the sting of the needle in the back of my neck.

I tensed up before I ripped the door open and ran for my life. I don't know how I got down the stairs or even how I managed to maneuver my liquid legs around the bodies littered everywhere. The sun was peeking through the windows and all I could think about was getting home. I couldn't trust Tracey, and I wasn't going to try to get into her car. A few miles wouldn't hurt. I could get there, even with my body feeling like this. All that mattered was getting home alive.

Fire slipped through my back where the needle

had struck me. Was this what heroin felt like? What was this feeling? I stumbled out of the frat house and onto the lawn. Rocks dug into my hands but I pushed myself back up and ran. My gait was slightly sideways but I continued on. A few joggers looked at me concerned as they passed me by but no one offered me help. I was sure I looked a fright but it didn't matter. I doubted I was the weirdest thing they had seen on a college campus before.

I leaned over and took a deep breath. My purse was gone and so was my phone. The only thing I had left was my watch on my wrist and my clothes. My panties were still in place which was good, I didn't think I needed to go to the police station. Though I had heard that they weren't much help around here. Me being drugged and possibly injected with who knows what wouldn't be at the top of their priority list. I had seen them turn away rape cases. I wasn't going to subject myself to any more humiliation. The last thing I wanted was for someone to not believe my story. I knew that happened more times than not. I swallowed back shame. I had done all of this to myself. I had put myself in the position and things could have gone so much worse. But at least I was alive...

One street after another and then another and I

was almost home. Sweat poured down my face as the sun continued its journey into the sky. I leaned against a tree and ran my hands down my tear-streaked face. I hadn't realized I had been crying. Even now, I hadn't stopped. My chest shuddered with a sob. I had been so incredibly stupid. I had trusted a bad boy and look at what had happened to me. I couldn't even remember the previous night. What if he had killed me? And Tracey... I had left Tracey with him. I looked back in the direction I came and felt my shoulders fall. No one was following me, I was almost home. Just a little more to go. I could make it.

CHAPTER 6

RAFE CRIMSON

"YOU DID WHAT?" Tracey exploded. She had picked up the half-empty syringe on the floor and threw it at me. "She will never trust you now."

"I did what I had to do, don't forget your place in this pack." I would have been lying to say I didn't feel guilty but what could I do? It had to happen. I couldn't put it off any longer. Every minute that passed meant that she wouldn't end up surviving the transformation if I didn't do it when I did.

A growl erupted from her chest and I managed to step out of the way right before she lunged at me with her half transformed claws. "She only got half of the venom! She will die."

I grabbed the little pink bag off of the bed and shoved it into Tracey's hands. "Make sure she gets this."

Tracey threw Jade's purse at my head. "She won't need any of these things now."

I caught the bag easily. "Maybe I can return it to her."

Tracey rolled her eyes. "Only if you plan on getting peppered with buckshot."

I shrugged. "It won't kill me."

CHAPTER 7
JADE RIVERS

When we had left my house the night before, I hadn't thought everything out as much as I imagined did. Especially how I was going to get back into my house. Climbing up onto the little roof above the dining room window was going to be difficult even if my body didn't feel like a noodle. I didn't have my key, it was tucked into the bottom pocket of my purse but even if I did, my parents would see my mascara streaked face. On top of that, my outfit was crooked and my hair was a fright. I didn't need them to worry any more than they already did.

It wasn't like I couldn't go out, I was an adult, but I didn't want them to feel like they had to be here. I didn't want them to worry about their adrenaline junky, danger loving child. So, I slumped my shoulders and took the long way to the woods that backed up to my house. The woods wouldn't be as scary in the daytime, would they?

They weren't. Light filtered through the branches and I didn't have to use the little amount of battery left on my watch to light the way. I wrapped my arms around myself and came out of the darkened area right behind my house.

The wood on the fence dug into my hands as I launched myself over the side of it. I hugged the side of the yard and tried to keep my breathing controlled. All I wanted to do was take off running as fast as I could. I needed the safety of my bedroom, the safety of my bed. It felt like an eternity had passed when I finally made it to the dining room window. I stared up at the side of the building I would need to climb in order to get back inside.

Thankfully there was a hose rack screwed to this side of the house. Though it didn't look very reliable. My boots slid around for a minute as I tried to get on top of it. My hands dug into the brick on the side of the house which didn't offer much help. When my boots stopped sliding and I felt like I had good enough balance on the hose rack, I jumped as hard as I could. My fingers made purchase with the lip on the gutter and for a moment, all I could do was hang there. The pain hardly registered through my hands even though the metal was definitely biting through my skin. I had never excelled at P.E. but I could manage a pull-up and this time, all I needed was one. My arms trembled as I slowly pulled my body up and over onto the little roof. My hands were slick with sweat and perspiration slid down my brow. The real challenge would be jumping sideways to my open window.

I backtracked slightly on the tiny patch of shingles to give myself the best chance at a running start. My heart stopped as I went airborne. My chest and stomach slammed into the stucco. I let out a wheeze as my fingers barely connected with the inside of my window. My arms were screaming now and my boots didn't have the right grip to help me up. They just slid down the stucco and the brick, like it was ice. My fingers inched toward the window sill and I was able to get the best grip I could manage to haul myself inside of my home. I flopped over the window sill and collapsed onto my bed. A strange smell tickled my nose. I prayed a wild animal hadn't gotten in overnight and died somewhere in my room.

But as I laid there on the floor I realized that the scent wasn't bad, in fact, it was incredible. It reminded me of pine trees and musk. With something else I couldn't quite put my finger on. I gave up and closed my eyes but then it registered that the light was on and I had remembered turning it off before we left the night before.

My legs shook as I stood up and my purse in the middle of my bed made me pause. I curled my fingers into fists. Had Tracey made it back before I had? It wasn't possible. She was clumsy and could hardly get out of the window to begin with. She would have died trying to get back up. There was a yellow sticky note waiting on top of it.

"Nice panties, try to not lose your bag next time. -R."

Rafe had drugged me. Tried to kill me and now he had been in my bedroom. I plucked the note from the outside of my bag and shredded it over the little garbage tin beside my desk. He was taunting me. I turned around in a little circle as I surveyed my room. My entire body shook still and the thought of him being in my room wasn't helping.

Was he still here? How did he know which house had been mine? Had he gone through the front door?

I flew across the room and fumbled with my zipper on my purse. I fumbled with the few contents in it before my fingers wrapped around my cell-phone. The screen flashed a battery symbol before it went dark. *No.* I plugged it into the charger and waited for it to boot up. I put my watch on its charger next. If my parents needed me they could still reach me on that. Then I realized something else.

The extra panties I had packed the night before, *just in case*, were missing too.

CHAPTER 8

RAFE CRIMSON

Scaling the side of Jade's home had been easy enough. Toying with her was fun. I watched from the woods as she freaked out over her missing panties and swirled them on my finger. Watching her squirm was worth it. Though it had been more entertaining to watch her struggling to get up the side of her house. The joys of being human. I didn't feel bad, nor did I feel envious of her humanity.

For the most part, humans disgusted me. Though they had their perks. They were great lays and even better playthings. I frowned. But this was different. Jade's mortality was hanging by a thread and I was possibly the one that put the nail right in her coffin.

It made me feel in a way I hadn't felt before. It made me sad and that was the one thing I never was.

I shoved her lace unmentionables into my pocket and walked through the center of the woods back to my home. A souvenir of sorts. A parting gift. After all, I had gone through *all* the trouble to get her things back to her.

CHAPTER 9
JADE RIVERS

No matter how many times I had watched the surveillance footage, I couldn't see Rafe on any of them. He had managed to evade all of the cameras and get into my room before I made it home. How had I missed him? Was I that exhausted? Had it really taken me that long to get home? A few miles didn't seem like a lot in my head, but in reality... It was a bit different. My brain had been so foggy.

I had waited for the effects of whatever drug Rafe had given me to kick in but they never did. My feet dragged as I made it into my bathroom and locked the door behind me. I couldn't bring myself to look in the mirror. I was too afraid of the broken girl I would see there. A sob worked its way up my throat again and I gritted my teeth. I wouldn't let him win. I wouldn't let any of them win. I peeled my clothes off of my body and shoved them into the garbage can. I never wanted to remember this day and the clothes, honestly, deserved to be burned but this was the best I could do. The hot water did little to make me feel clean. Even after scrubbing my body raw, I still felt dirty. I still felt wrong and unclean. I wrapped a towel around myself and tried to keep the tears away. They would do nothing for me. I slid my curtains closed and my hands shook as I pulled pajamas on.

Text messages pinged through on my phone but the only ones I answered were from my parents. Their flight was delayed because of bad weather and they would be a few more days. I didn't know if I was relieved or terrified. I no longer wanted to be alone. Tracey was the sender of the other texts, but I didn't care. I deleted them immediately without reading them. She had warned me about running, but it didn't matter, she was still in on it somehow.

So, I stayed like that. Wrapped up in my covers like they would protect me from the big bad boy I had gotten myself tangled up with. The only time I left the bed was when I had started to sweat and then nausea rolled through me. Maybe the effects of the drugs were finally starting to kick in.

After throwing up a few times, I felt better and made myself go down to the kitchen to eat. I hadn't gone to the store earlier in the week and now I was growing to regret it. My stomach growled.

My phone buzzed with another text. Tracey- "*Can we talk?*"

I rolled my eyes and tossed the phone onto the counter. What could I possibly have to say to her?

Then it popped into my head. I had a few choice words for her. She wasn't going to get away with what had happened to me.

Me- "*Lose my number, my address, and every memory you have of me.*"

Tracey- "*It's not what you think. I can explain. How are you feeling?*"

I didn't bother with that. How could it not be what I thought? I had been drugged, then Rafe had tried to hurt me further or drug me further, then he had been in my bedroom. I didn't even want to think about the panties he jacked. I typed out a quick text to my parents, letting them know I was feeling a tad sick but would be better in a few days. Hopefully by the time they got back home.

I dug through my freezer and came across a couple of steaks. My family wasn't big on red meat. I had practically been vegetarian my entire life but now my mouth was salivating at thought of rare steaks. I licked my lips as I tossed them into the sink and turned the water on to defrost them.

My stomach clenched and nausea rolled through me again. I managed to rush to the half-bath in the hallway by the kitchen in time. My socks slid on the tiled floors as I skidded to a stop in front of the door. I ripped it open just as vomit expelled from my stomach. I don't know how I even made it to the toilet. My body sagged against the wall and I prayed this was it.

On quaking legs, I stumbled from the bathroom and back to the kitchen. I placed both of my hands on either side of the sink and splashed my clammy face with the cold water.

Ding.

Another text.

Tracey- "*Are you feeling okay? I'm really worried about you. If you get sick please let me come take care of you.*"

Me- "*How can I possibly trust you now?*"

Tracey- "*I'm the only one you have ever trusted to go out with you and let you get completely turnt. Yes, I admit I know Rafe, but he's more of a family friend than anything else. I saw him give you a drink and kept my eyes on both of you all night. I tried to keep him away from you. You have to understand that I would never condone what happened last night."*

Me- *"Then help me press charges."*

I didn't want to press charges. I didn't know why but the whole situation had been weird. But I needed to know what she would say to that. Especially since they were family friends.

Tracey- *"You can try but family's like Rafe's have old money. I don't think it'll turn out the way you want it to. The police in this town are corrupt. Have you told your parents yet?"*

There it was. The reason I ultimately couldn't go to the police. In the grand scheme of things, it would only make my life harder and I would possibly have to change schools. This would all end in an explosion. An explosion I wasn't ready for. An explosion I would never be ready for.

I turned the sink off and processed the texts Tracey had sent. Could she really be innocent in all of this? She did tell me to run. She had probably been the reason that things hadn't escalated after he drugged me.

The steaks sizzled and popped as I placed them in a skillet on the gas stovetop. My stomach rumbled again as I flipped the meat. I had never cooked a steak before, but I did love a cooking show on Youtube. I had thankfully picked up a few tips.

I typed out a text to Tracey. "*I will think about forgiving you. I'm feeling fine.*"

Tracey- "*If things get bad, just please, let me help you. This is serious and I don't want you to go through this alone. You know how my grandma is with her witchy concoctions. She's been begging me to bring you one.*"

I didn't say anything back. My steaks were finished. I didn't know how I knew but I did. If they continued to cook they would be nasty and the thought of well-done meat turned my stomach again.

The first taste of the meat about sent me over the edge. The nausea that had been swimming around my body was gone with that first bite. I tore through both steaks in a manner that would have given my mother a heart attack. I usually had manners but something else took over. Something animalistic inside of me tore through the food at a breakneck pace. Through the haze of shame and bitterness from the night before and the sickness that had been plaguing me, I didn't seem to care about any of it anymore.

CHAPTER 10
JADE RIVERS

Days had passed and I still wasn't getting any better. The only thing that made me feel remotely fine was meat. But the only problem with that was every single smell set me off. I had walked into the grocery store and had to run right out. The trash can at the front of the store was now full of my vomit. I didn't know what the smell was that had turned my stomach so badly, but it was overwhelming. Like baby powder.

So when I attempted my second trip, I had made sure to wrap a scarf around the bottom half of my face. Maybe it would keep people away so I wouldn't get them sick too. It barely masked the smell of the people milling in and out of the building, but it allowed me to get to the meat department without throwing up again.

The first scent of meat was scary. I had almost torn the fabric from my face and shoved the hamburger meat down my throat right there. Raw. By the grace of all things holy, I got through checkout and back home without any more strange incidents. Was this what mad cow was like? Was I dying? How on earth was I feeling this way? Was it the drugs Rafe had injected me with? Even though it had been days since?

I slammed the meat into a pot on the stove and stared at my phone. Oh, how I wished I had his number. All I wanted to do was give him a piece of my mind and possibly punch him in the face. No, I definitely was going to punch him in the face. All I had to do was go to another party. All I wanted to know was why and what he had injected into me? That was it and then maybe I could punch him in the throat.

But could I actually do that now? Did I have the guts to subject myself to a party again? The thought of a party no longer ignited my soul. The thought of a party didn't seem so fun anymore. Whatever high I got from going out was gone now. Rafe had ruined that. Rafe had ruined me. But I wasn't going to let him get away with it. He had taken my fun and now I was going to take his. I just needed to figure out what it was. Drugging girls? I would show him how fun it wasn't to be the victim. I wasn't going to let him do this to someone else.

For the first time in days, I felt something like hope. Revenge would do that to you. I smiled as I stirred the browning meat, then I realized there was hardly any pink left and I ripped the pot from the stove. Something was definitely wrong with me.

Raw meat should have horrified me. It would have any other day before. But... the smell was entirely too heavenly.

The only problem was stepping a foot outside of my house and expecting to not get sick. Every single smell set me on edge. So much so that I doubted my period that I had a few weeks before. Every symptom I looked up led me right to pregnancy, but there was no way that was plausible.

School was no longer an option and I was thanking my lucky stars that Tracey was still trying to be my friend. She made sure to email me each of my assignments and if she didn't have a class with me, she found a friend that did. Even though I was still somewhat frustrated with her, I couldn't help but feel grateful even if it was probably her fault that I was sick in the first place.

I really couldn't win. This was all a disaster. My

phone vibrated and I expected to see a text but instead, it was a phone call from my mom.

"Hello?"

"Hey, honey! How are you feeling?" Her voice blasted through the speakers. I winced and dropped my phone in surprise. The volume on my phone wasn't even turned up all the way and the speaker option wasn't turned on either.

This time I didn't press the phone to my ear and held it a healthy distance from my face. "I'm getting better."

I eyed the bowl of half-raw meat. Could I even say I was getting better? Something was wrong with my brain.

"Your voice doesn't sound like it, are you sure you don't want us to come back sooner?" My dad was saying something in the background but I couldn't make it out. The speaker sounded like it was in a tunnel now. I squeezed my eyes closed and tried to focus on anything else besides the piercing sound coming from my phone.

"What's wrong with my voice?" I asked then added quickly. "I don't want either of you to get sick too. This is miserable."

"You sound," she paused. "I don't know, growly?

But besides that, you need someone to take care of you!"

I couldn't risk them coming home and seeing me eat raw meat. So I lied. "No, that's okay, Tracey is taking care of me."

"Oh, that's weird, we haven't seen her on the cameras." Leave it to my parents to catch me in a lie.

"Well, she's getting my assignments for me and she's coming over tomorrow to help me with some stuff." I sighed. I would have to invite Tracey over. What could go wrong?

CHAPTER 11
RAFE CRIMSON

I stared at Tracey from across the dinner table. "What do you mean she invited you over?"

She rolled her caramel-colored eyes. "You heard me. She forgave me."

I narrowed my eyes at her and pushed my food away from me. "Not when she realizes what you *are*."

She smirked. "You think she will want to have anything to do with you when she finds out who *we* are?"

"Things will be different then."

Tracey gave me and everyone else a fake smile. We didn't normally have formal dinners with the entire pack, but tonight was the night before the full moon. It was a celebration of sorts. It gave us a chance to be a pack while human before we ran the next night. The next night that Tracey wouldn't be running with the rest of the pack. Which was dangerous but she was needed elsewhere. There wasn't much I could argue with that. I could give the order for her to stay back but it wouldn't do anything but hurt Jade. That was the last thing I wanted to do. But I had to keep my distance.

Tracey's father sat back in his chair and looked between us. "Is this about that girl again?"

Axel had been my father's right-hand man, and now he was mine. I gritted my teeth in annoyance. "Yes, her name is Jade."

His dark brows rose up his dark chocolate forehead. "Humans are finicky creatures. She will not handle our secret well."

Tracey looked down at her plate as her mother wrapped her cream arms around Tracey's waist. "They aren't children anymore, Axel. They can handle a lot more than we give them credit for."

I would have loved to hear what my father would have said about the situation but fortunately, I had put him in his grave a few years prior. He wouldn't have liked any of this just as much as Axel didn't. But it wasn't any of Axel's business. I didn't need Axel's permission to do anything in *my* pack.

CHAPTER 12
JADE RIVERS

Sunlight streamed through my bedroom window and pierced my eyes through my eyelids. I kicked the blankets off of my legs and stretched. I didn't feel as sick this morning as I had in the last week. My eyes burned though and that wasn't normal. The light coming in through the window was a lot brighter than it had been on previous mornings. I blinked my eyes several times in hopes that it would stop the pain.

I rubbed my fists into my eyes but it just made it worse. My legs maneuvered me to the bathroom even though I couldn't see. Sleeping in my contacts was a usual thing, but they weren't agreeing with me today. I kept the lights off as I pulled my eyelids open and scraped the plastic lens off of my eyeballs. I leaned against the counter and finally opened my eyes. The burning was gone but something was different. The room looked like the lights were dimmed. But we didn't have dimmable lighting in the bathrooms and I hadn't turned the lights on either.

I squeezed my eyes shut before I opened them again and again. Nothing changed. I ripped the bedroom door open and I could see in perfect clarity. Even better than I had with my contacts in.

Was this a side effect of the drug? Did it somehow mutate and cure my partial blindness? This could be a good thing. I shook my head. Nothing about Rafe was a good thing, including the drug he had given me without my consent.

But then the doorbell rang and my ears were flooded with intense pain from the sound. What was happening to me?

I pulled a sweatshirt from the top of my dresser and hoped I wouldn't smell anything that would make me throw up again. I didn't bother with changing out of my leggings from the night before and pulled my long blonde hair into a bun on the top of my head. As I galloped down the stairs, I could hear something tapping against the ground outside. It wasn't until I yanked the front door open that I realized it was Tracey tapping her foot on the front doorstep. My eyes zeroed in on the sandals she was wearing. They seemed extra sparkly. In fact, everything seemed to be brighter, clearer, and just plain vibrant. Her mustard-colored sweater seemed to glow.

The smell of Tracey didn't revolt me either. She smelled of fresh-cut grass and something floral. I hadn't noticed it before. "Did you get a new perfume?"

She frowned and lifted her arm for a sniff. "No, I don't think so. Why? Do I smell funny?"

I shrugged. "I don't know, everything has smelled funny lately. You're the first thing that smells *normal.*"

She smiled at me and pushed her way past me into the foyer. "How have you been feeling?"

"I've had better days."

I followed her down the hall and to the kitchen. She put her backpack in the center of the white island. The sound of the zipper was almost too loud. I winced. She dug around in the bag for a minute before she pulled a Mason Jar from its depths.

Inside of the jar was a greenish, brown muck. It looked to be as thick as peanut butter. Just the sight of it made my stomach roll. "What's that?"

She smiled at me like she had finally gotten my

friendship back and things were back to the way they were before I was drugged. But they weren't and they never would be. I didn't know if I could even trust her. The only reason she was here was because I needed to get my parents off my back. She slid the jar across the countertop and then dug a spoon out of the drawer in front of her.

"This will help you feel better. You need to eat a spoonful of this every morning until it's gone."

I was too afraid to open it. I had a feeling the smell was worse than its appearance. A few seconds ticked away and Tracey realized I wasn't going to open it. I could have sworn a twinkle lit up in her eye as she slid the jar back toward herself and popped the top. I cringed as I waited for the scent to hit my nose.

No smell came from the open jar. I peered at it suspiciously. How odd. Maybe Tracey's grandmother really was a witch. The spoon moved through the mixture easily as I scooped some up. The mixture was heavy on my tongue but didn't have a taste. It was hard to swallow it down but after it was completely gone from my mouth, I realized all the sensitivities I was having to light and sound were gone.

Yep, Tracey's grandma was definitely a witch.

CHAPTER 13
JADE RIVERS

It was easy to forgive Tracey. Everything she did was selfless and I should have seen that from the start when she didn't get smashed when we went out together. She always made sure I was in her sights and she never left without me or without telling me where she was going. I never felt uneasy when I was with her. She was the kind of friend that I had taken advantage of and now that I thought about it... I realized how much I didn't deserve her before. She had always helped me and put me first and I had never done the same for her. Tracey was the kind of friend I wanted to be.

So what happened with Rafe made everything all the weirder. I couldn't understand the connection of family friends because my parents had never had anyone close to them like that. They had moved on from high school and didn't bring any of their friends with them. Their journey of infertility alienated them from many people along the way. I was pretty certain I didn't even have godparents, which was fine. I preferred to do things alone. So understanding the loyalty that came with family or even family friends was foreign to me. I hadn't even had a best friend growing up. I didn't go to dance class or have extracurricular activities to keep me busy. I usually stayed glued to my parents with a book in my hand. I didn't mind it... but it did get lonely at times.

But Tracey had swooped me up under her protective wing and hadn't let me go since freshman year. I called her my friend loosely, but out of all of the people I could count on... She was the only one.

Which, honestly, when admitting that to myself, it seemed really pathetic. My parents were both only children and their parents had died while I was still in diapers. It made sense that I stayed alone, but now? Now not so much.

Tracey spun around in my office chair and eyed me curiously. "What really made you want me to come over? It couldn't have been your own free will to decide your immediate forgiveness."

I leaned against my headboard and pulled at a

string on my comforter. "You're right, I lied to my parents and I needed proof to back up my words. I don't want them to worry about me. The last thing I need is for them to ask questions about my weekend from hell."

Tracey toyed with her messy curls and wouldn't meet my eyes. "There are so many things I wish I could tell you about that night, but just know this, I wasn't involved in Rafe drugging you or even injecting you with more sedative."

"That was sedative?" I guess that made sense. If he wanted to do anything else he would have needed me to stay asleep. Did that mean nothing from the syringe had made it into my system? "What were you a part of then?"

She leaned back and the chair tilted with her body weight. Her bright teeth snagged her bottom lip and for a second it looked like they were longer and pointier than usual. "I was involved in trying to hook you two up. But I knew you weren't looking for anything long term and figured the timing was off. Rafe has unconventional methods."

"Why did he drug me?"

Tracey shrugged. "I honestly couldn't tell ya. I haven't really spoken to him much about it."

I raised my eyebrows. "You've spoken to him since this all happened?"

Tracey rolled her head on her shoulders. She wouldn't look me in the eyes again. "We probably shouldn't talk about this. If you'd like, I can leave. I only want to make sure you're okay."

I shook my head and tears welled up in my eyes. "I am not okay. I have been feeling weird since the entire thing and I came to the realization today that I am always alone. I *hate* being alone. I never realized it before because I blanketed the feeling under partying and adrenaline. But now I'm forced to look at my feelings and right now I'm feeling pretty lousy. You can go if you want but you're probably the only one I have ever cared about besides my parents." I closed my eyes and sighed before I opened them up again and admitted defeat. "I don't want to be alone. I'm scared."

Tracey unfolded herself from the desk chair and sat next to me on the bed. "I don't really care for Rafe all that much but we grew up together. Side by side. Everyone thought we were going to end up mat-married. When his dad died he went through a lot and my parents have been there for him ever since." She pulled my hand into hers. "I don't want you to think I'm sticking up for him or hanging out with

him because of what he did. I want you to understand that I can't exactly shake Rafe Crimson. He
lives next door to me."

"Crimson?" I frowned. "Isn't that the oldest
family in the town? Like everything around here is
named after them?"

The mascot of the university was the Crimson
Coyotes. The library had the Crimson Crest stamped
into the front double doors. It had a wolf's face
stamped on the front of a shield with two spears
crossed behind it. Everyone knew who the Crimson's
were.

Tracey leaned back and nodded. Her wild curls
bunched up against the headboard and her nose
wrinkled. "Yeah, that's the one. Rafe, his little
brother, and his mom are the only Crimsons left."

"Don't try to make me feel bad for him. Just
because he lost someone doesn't mean he's a decent
human."

Tracey snorted. "Oh, he's definitely not a decent
human, but he has his quirks. Maybe someday he
will show you that he's not as bad as he looks or
sometimes acts."

I closed my eyes. I couldn't believe I was about to
tell her this. "He stole my panties."

Tracey laughed. "No, he didn't. I saw him hand

you that cup then followed him upstairs when he had you in his arms. I made sure he didn't touch you indecently. Though, I know he would never do that."

I bit the inside of my cheek. "No, like he stole my extra pair I kept in my purse."

Tracey's burst of laughter almost had me jumping out of my skin. Heat filled my face. "Are you serious? When I told him to return your things, I didn't think he would go through them."

"This isn't funny," I grumbled.

"I can't wait to tear him apart for that one." Laughter continued to spill from her lips. For the first time since that night, I felt normal again, even if I didn't feel whole yet.

CHAPTER 14
JADE RIVERS

As the sun had gone down I watched as Tracey went from energetic to nervous. We had spent the entire day together and nothing got old. I could listen to her tell stories for hours. Stories about her growing up in the woods or how her parents raised her with all their friends. They had the tightest community and she loved every second of it. There were even a few endearing stories about Rafe thrown in. But that didn't mean I wasn't going to enact my revenge. He had it coming for him and I couldn't wait to deliver justice.

As her nerves continued to go up, her eyes started to glow. I wanted to think it was only my imagination but when she asked to stay the night, I was worried about her. Her eyes were almost yellow and her voice had gotten a little deeper. I had asked her several times if she was okay and she had reassured me that she was. I didn't believe her. But I was thankful she stayed, I didn't feel like going through another night alone. Crying myself to sleep wasn't something I enjoyed doing. Having her around kept me from the pits of my own despair.

When the pain shot through my body, I was especially grateful to have her beside me. I shot up in the bed and pain spiraled down my spine.

Tracey flicked the light on, but it didn't matter. I could see in the dark now. Which was the least surprising thing that had happened lately.

Pain shot down my fingers before my teeth felt like they were going to fall out. Every single nerve ending in my body felt like it was on fire. All I could do was writhe in the bed. I whimpered as Tracey pushed my hair from my face.

Another wave of pain hit me and I shot off of the bed. What now? I cried out as more pain took over my body. I knew I was going to die. This was it and I was going to accept it. The syringe hadn't had a sedative in it, it had something that was going to kill me slowly. I knew it.

"I'm so sorry," I managed to get out.

"For what?" Tracey asked as she came in from

the bathroom. She pressed a cool cloth against my forehead and I felt myself relax slightly.

"For being a jerk to you," My back shot off of the bed again as the pain came back even worse.

"That's the last thing I'm worried about." She continued to wash my face even as I thrashed on the bed.

Another cry escaped my lips. "Please, tell my parents that I love them."

"You aren't dying, Jade." Tracey's voice was stern. There was no arguing with her right now.

I could have sworn I heard her say, "Your first change is always the hardest." But that was the least of my worries as darkness overtook me.

CHAPTER 15
JADE RIVERS

A night I couldn't remember and a splitting headache. Too bad I knew that the two weren't from a good time. Bits and pieces of the night before filtered through my head as I blinked my eyes open. Then I immediately closed them tightly. Something bad had happened. My room was trashed and Tracey was curled up at the foot of my bed. She had a cut along her cheek and blood on her shirt.

"You have to face the music eventually," Tracey grumbled.

"I'm still sleeping," I replied back tiredly.

Tracey shifted at my feet and jostled the bed. Aches and pains rolled through my joints. There was soreness in places I didn't know I could be sore in. I peeked my eyes back open and Tracey stared at me from the end of the bed.

"How'd you sleep?" Her eyes were no longer glowing but the cut on her cheek was making me nervous.

I looked around at my destroyed bedroom. "What happened here?"

Tracey pushed her wild hair from her eyes and winced. "I don't know if I'm the right person to talk to about all of this."

"What does that mean?" I crossed my arms over my chest and realized I was bleeding too. There were claw marks up and down my arms. I shoved the blankets from my legs and stood up. My clothes were shredded on the floor. "What did you do to me?'

Tracey's lips pressed together in a thin line. "You did this to me." She held her hand up and touched the tender spot on her face.

I reared back as if I had been slapped. "I didn't do that to you."

Tracey rolled her eyes and pulled her bag from the floor. "Yes, you did. You probably remember nothing from last night but I can tell you that it was rough. Hell, just look under your rug."

She grabbed her bag and went into the bathroom. A few seconds later the shower cranked on and steam rolled under the door. I sighed and rolled the rug out of the way. Sure enough, there were deep gouges in the floor next to the bed. It looked like an animal had gone insane in here. There were claw marks everywhere. I raked my fingers through my hair but stopped short as discomfort ran through my fingertips.

The tips of my fingers were raw and bloody. Some of the nails were even cracked or broken off. I rubbed my hands down the shirt covering myself. The hem of it hit my knees and the collar was stretched and hanging down off of my shoulder.

The water stopped in the bathroom and after a few minutes, Tracey emerged with a towel around her head. The gash on her cheek wasn't as ugly but it definitely needed stitches. How had I managed to do that to her? She threw herself down onto the bed and watched me curiously.

"Last night shouldn't have happened the way it did." She buried her face in her hands. "If I had known, I would have brought you to my parents."

My head was spinning. "Talk after I get out of the shower."

Tracey refused to talk about anything until we got to her parent's house. Which I wasn't too excited about, to begin with. But if it would get me answers, I wouldn't turn the opportunity down. I had never met her parents, mainly because she lived in a dorm on campus. She spoke of her grandmother often and I knew she lived nearby. But when we drove into the woods that backed up to my house I could feel my anxiety skyrocket. The little dirt road brought us to a massive iron gate that had the Crimson Crest stamped into it. I had figured Rafe and Tracey's parents were neighbors in a *neighborhood,* not living on a commune in the middle of the woods. This was an awful idea. I clutched the door handle, ready to bolt if I needed to.

I pushed my wet hair from my face and sat up straighter. Even though the movement made my back ache, I stayed that straight until a house popped up in the distance. It was a work of art. It had to be at least five thousand square feet. It was an old farmhouse that looked like it had been remodeled. The full wrap around porch almost had me drooling. The white paint was shiny in the sunlight as we pulled up in front of it. There were various cars parked around it. I refused to acknowledge all of the expensive cars around us.

I forced my mouth closed and looked at Tracey with a shocked expression. "Everyone lives here?"

She shook out her curls. "No, this is just the main house. Behind the house is another dirt road that will bring you to the other homes here. This is just our common ground where we go to eat dinner, have game night, or just not feel so alone."

Which sounded amazing for someone that was as lonely as I was. But all of it was foreign. What was it like to be loved by so many? To never have to worry about not having love from someone? One look at the white crest stamped onto the glass on the front door and I had a bad feeling about who owned the main house. I was rooted in my seat, even after Tracey shut the car off and got out.

Even though she closed her door, I could still hear her when she spoke. "I don't think he's here."

And somehow, I knew that was a lie.

CHAPTER 16
RAFE CRIMSON

Tracey had warned me she was coming with Jade. Even though I had been prepared, nothing helped with the feelings that spiked in my chest as I watched her refuse to get out of Tracey's car. She crossed her torn up arms over her chest and her bottom lip jutted out. I wasn't even going to try to tell myself that it wasn't adorable. But that was the last thing I needed to be thinking. They were here for a reason. Everything that should have happened last night, didn't. That meant me and Tracey's parents were on clean up duty.

Axel was going to be pissed. I hadn't told him what I had done and when he found out, he wasn't going to take too kindly to it. I had a feeling there would be a challenge over it. Which was fine, pack challenges happened all the time when the wolves got anxious or even angry with the dynamic that I enforced.

Jade finally shoved the car door open and walked up the front porch on shaking legs. I could hear the rapid pace of her heartbeat through the floor under my feet. It was time to face the music. Jade Rivers was about to get the surprise of a lifetime.

CHAPTER 17
JADE RIVERS

Tracey's father, Axel, didn't look very pleased to meet me. His massive hand shook mine but the frown on his face never left. He was a handsome man and I could see where Tracey got some of her looks from. His big brown eyes looked like he would possibly be a softy if you caught him on the right day. Today was clearly not that day. After Tracey introduced me to him, her mother came down the stairs next. She was the opposite of Axel. She was soft and kind where Axel was brooding and unforgiving with his stance. Her skin was soft and translucent where Axel's was dark and rich. They were the perfect yin and yang.

Instead of shaking my hand, Vivian hugged me. She smelled like flowers and mud. Which was odd.

Tracey took a deep breath and led me over to the massive wooden table beside the kitchen. It was breathtaking. The renovations the home had gone through had been recent. Walls had been knocked down and large wooden beams took up their placements on the ceiling. The table had enough seating for fifty people, at least. Did they have that many people living on this property? *How strange.*

Vivian opened her mouth to speak when I smelled it. *Him.* The heavenly smell that had taken over my bedroom like he had rolled across every inch of it that day he had returned my belongings. The scent still lingered even a week later. Pine needles, musk, and something spicier. Something hotter. My stomach clenched and I had to curl my hands into fists to get the hot feelings to go away. I hated this place already.

When Rafe entered the room, I jumped from my seat and lunged for him. No one saw it coming. Not even Rafe. My fist flew and knocked him right in the nose. Blood sprayed and I went in for another punch. This one was anticipated. He grabbed my fist in a tight hold and glared down into my eyes. I glared back. He wasn't going to intimidate me. He was the one that had created this entire mess, I was sure of it. He didn't wipe the blood flowing down his face as he stared into my eyes. I gritted my teeth as I swung my other hand. The sound of my slap rang through the room. He didn't even blink. I continued to stare into his yellow eyes and growled.

There was a collected gasp behind me but it didn't make me back down. No, it made me want to take him down even more.

"You need to stop this, Jade, you don't know the war you are waging. This can get dangerous." Tracey's voice came out as a growl behind me and it snapped me out of it. I turned away from Rafe and frowned at the family staring at us. Their expressions were shell shocked. Something like victory rolled through me. I felt powerful.

"You've got guts, Jade," Rafe said as he released my hand and slid into the chair at the head of the table. "I'll give you that."

"You won't have any if you keep talking to me," I sneered.

Axel looked between us and shook his head. "What is going on here?"

I smiled as I tattled on the stupid man staring at me. "Rafe drugged me last weekend and tried to continue to drug me after I woke up."

Tracey made a face like she wanted to explain but she couldn't. She just leaned back in her chair and Axel took the floor. "What the hell happened?"

Rafe looked between us all with a satisfied smirk

on his face. I wanted to claw it off. "Jade likes bad boys, so I showed her just how bad I can be."

Axel narrowed his eyes at both of us. I wasn't going to deny the fact that I had liked bad boys, it would have been a lie and I didn't like lies unless they were completely necessary. It wasn't vital in this current situation.

A growl rumbled through the room and Axel slammed his hands down on the table. "So you thought it would be a good idea to turn her?"

"Turning her would mean that I would have had to claim her," Rafe picked at his nails like this was the most boring thing he had ever had to do. "I didn't claim her, in case you're wondering."

Turn? My brain went ninety to nothing with that term. What was happening? What did this mean?

"I can tell you didn't claim her," Axel pinched the bridge of his nose in agitation. "I just can't understand why you would turn her, without the approval of the pack first."

Rafe shrugged. "As Alpha, I wasn't aware of the fact that I must pass everything by the pack. This doesn't endanger the pack."

Axel exploded then. "The hell it doesn't!"

Vivian put her hand on her husband's. He managed to control his rage with her help. "Rafe, honey, you know the rules. Unless she is dying of injuries inflicted by the pack or your true mate, turning isn't allowed."

What. The. Hell.

Tracey's eyes found mine and she smiled. I could tell it was meant to be reassuring. I felt anything but reassured. What kind of mess had I allowed myself to get caught up in?

Rafe shrugged again. "As Alpha, I also don't have to explain anything at the moment. When further information becomes available, I will clue you all in. Is that all? I have a date this evening."

"Try not to drug her too." If looks could kill he would have been dead.

Rafe cocked an eyebrow and pushed his chair back. The legs on his chair scraped across the floor with a loud screech that had me cringing. "Baby, I did a lot worse than drug you. Enjoy the shit show."

With that, he got up and flounced out of the room. Axel's face was beet red from barely controlled rage and Vivian had a strange, confused look on her face. They both looked at Tracey for answers and all she did was grin. Except, it wasn't a grin, she was baring her teeth.

This was great, just freaking fantastic.

CHAPTER 18
JADE RIVERS

Hours passed and I was still no closer to the information I needed. My body was humming with frustration. I wanted to leave and go home but as much as I wanted to, I knew it wasn't going to happen. Tracey walked me around the property and to her parent's home. She talked about how there was an acre of land for her to build her house here one day and I wondered about the word *pack* that everyone had kept throwing around. Here I sat with unanswered questions and more confusion swirling in my head.

We passed a waterfall and I sighed. "Tracey, please take me home."

"Your body is going through some changes right now," She chewed on her lip.

I rolled my eyes. "I don't think having the birds and the bees talk is really going to help me here."

Tracey grabbed my hand into her honey-colored one. "No really. Last night and everything that happened, I think your brain is suppressing the memories because it was too traumatic. Your first shift shouldn't have been like that."

"Everyone keeps saying that and pack and I don't know what the hell is happening!" I yanked my hand out of her hers and marched away. My boots crunched on the leaves beneath my feet.

Tracey stayed rooted in her spot. "You're a werewolf."

I blinked a few times before I turned around. She continued talking, "Last night was the full moon and I knew you would be partially shifting, but I guess my wolf triggered yours."

My world shifted. I felt like I was going to fall sideways. I blinked a few times. I knew weird things were happening, but a werewolf? A freaking wolf? I pressed my hands to my chest and tried to control my rapid breaths. If I wasn't careful, I was going to pass out right there. I ran my hands down the front of my jeans and shook my head. Nope. Nope. I wouldn't accept this. How the hell did this even happen? Bile rose up my throat. But then hysteria won over and I laughed. I actually laughed.

"What happened? Did Rafe have something to do with this?" My knees gave out and I fell to the leafy floor. I buried my hands into the dirt as I tried to control my breathing.

"With the needle." She sat down beside me. "He didn't want to claim you."

"What does that mean?" I couldn't even wrap my mind around the fact that she said I was a werewolf. A freaking werewolf. What the hell?

"Take you as his mate." She chewed on her plush bottom lip again before her hand found mine. She held it loosely in hers and I didn't have the strength to pull away from her comfort.

"Mate?" I asked. I thought I knew what she meant but I had to be sure.

"A forever union between two people that our wolves choose. They choose compatible wolves or partners that will make strong pups and protect them if needed."

It shouldn't have bothered me that he didn't think I was qualified to be mate material for him but it stung a little. I was clearly delusional. He had drugged me, turned me, and then he had snubbed me. This was all fantastic. Best news ever. *Not*.

"How do I know this isn't all some joke orchestrated by the Prince Asshole himself?"

Tracey grinned. "First, I love that nickname for him. Second, I'll show you."

She yanked her shirt over her head then her pants down her legs. In seconds she was standing there nude like stripping in the woods was completely normal. Or... it was for her. But then she was on all fours and her body was stretching and contorting. Fur the same color as her hair sprouted all over her body. A growl erupted from my throat and I blinked in surprise. There was a weird stirring in my chest as Tracey's body finished its transformation. Standing almost as tall as I was, was a wolf with caramel coloring and bright yellow eyes. I stumbled backwards and fell onto my already sore bottom. Everything kept getting better and better.

She sat down on her hind legs and blinked slowly. I pressed my lips together. "So what do we do now?" She laid down on her front paws and blinked again. "I can't communicate with you, I don't know what to do. You proved a point."

"She can't transform again for a little bit." A little voice behind me made me jump.

I peered over my shoulder and came face to face with a little boy that couldn't be over the age of eight.

He was a little thing. His orange eyes glowed. He had dark hair that flopped over his forehead and slightly into his bright eyes.

"Why is that?" I asked.

He shrugged. "It takes a lot out of our bodies to transform into our wolves. It's not an easy feat."

I licked my lips. "No, I suppose not. I'm Jade."

He smiled and there was a huge gap between his front teeth. "I know, the whole pack is talking about you."

I nodded my head. *Of course.*

"I'm Ford," he held his hand out and I took it in mine. His scent was slightly familiar but I couldn't place it.

"So we can shift on command?" I found myself asking.

He teetered his head back and forth. "Kind of, our shift is stronger on a full moon though. She's not going to recover as quickly from this shift as she would have last night or if she was shifting with the rest of the pack."

I nodded my head. "Do you go to school?"

"We're homeschooled until we can control our shifts." He watched Tracey with me. "Around middle school."

"I guess it's not too funny to have a kindergartener transform in a class full of kids." I tried not to laugh at the picture in my mind. Maybe I could accept this as my new reality, but there was still nausea swirling around inside of me. I mean, I had to accept it, there was a werewolf sitting in front of me... but maybe, it wasn't so bad.

He shrugged as the corner of his mouth lifted up in a sideways grin. "Yeah, it's happened."

Tracey's body started to contort again and Ford smiled at me before he turned to leave. "Nice to meet you, Ford."

CHAPTER 19
RAFE CRIMSON

"She really isn't that bad," my little brother, Ford, muttered at the dinner table later that night. He pinched off a piece of his bread and made a face. He was getting closer to being able to control his shifts. I was surprised he had even entertained the thought of sides or extras besides the rare steak on his plate. Children usually preferred the red meat over anything else and then the rest of their palate developed later in life.

I rolled my eyes openly but inside was cringing. I couldn't let on what I knew. It would cause too many issues. Granted the ass-chewing I had gotten from Axel hadn't been a good one. He would have never done anything like that in front of the rest of the pack but I allowed it when we were alone. When we counseled on things regarding the pack. I valued his opinion and insight, even though it did rake my nerves. He had been second hand to the Alpha a lot longer than I had been alive.

But war was brewing and I couldn't even trust my second. Which didn't make anything easier either.

Poor Jade was going to end up right in the middle of it.

"Yeah?" I asked. "What do you know about girls, anyway?"

"I know that if you're nice to them, they'll be nice to you and they won't punch you in the nose or try to kill you."

"What if I tell you that this wasn't because I did anything?" I waved at my slightly crooked nose and bruising. She packed a wicked punch. This girl was going to be a seriously dangerous problem.

Ford laughed. "I wouldn't believe you."

"Hmmm," I scratched at the stubble on my jaw. "Glad you know me too well."

Ford balled up his little fist and punched me in the arm. I barely felt it. "You're too bad for someone like her. You should probably stay away before she finishes you off."

"Don't I know it, buddy."

CHAPTER 20

JADE RIVERS

The need to shift always came with an itch in my chest. It almost felt like a sneeze or an itch I couldn't scratch. I was scared to go back to the university without being able to shift or knowing if I would do it randomly. But every time I felt the need, I would close my eyes and picture myself hitting Rafe in the face and the feeling went away. Even though I hadn't shifted since the full moon, classes and life carried on like Rafe Crimson hadn't tried to steal it away. Everything continued like he wasn't the biggest thorn in my side.

Every evening after I was done with classes, Tracey would swing by the house and we would cook together while she schooled me on everything werewolf. It made it easier than me going back to the Crimson property. Or as Tracey called it, the

Crimson Pack. I was too much of a wild card and couldn't be trusted to not attack their Alpha again. Which, whatever, I didn't want to go there anyway. This worked well in my favor.

Though every few days I would peer out my window and I knew he was there, in the woods, behind my house. It didn't make me scared but only angry. He was lucky I wasn't going around the pack. I was practically out for blood with that one. If he kept it up I would search him out. I didn't like him lurking.

We were eating steaks, mostly raw, when Tracey brought up the pack life. Much to my disapproval, I let her continue on with the nonsense. "You're going to need a pack."

I rolled my eyes. "Says who?"

"Says the wolf inside of you." Tracey took a big bite out of her steak before she scooped up some mashed potatoes. She reassured me that I would crave regular food again soon, but I had my doubts about that. Just the look of the potatoes had my stomach rolling. "When you do get control over your shifts she will go rogue if you don't pledge to an Alpha."

"What does that even mean? I have to bow down to Rafe and just be happy that he hates me and I hate him?" I wasn't okay with that. I wasn't okay with bowing down to the man that had done this to me. The man that had tried to take everything from me. No, I wouldn't bow down to him, or anyone else. I could still be an independent bad-ass woman without an Alpha, right?

She shrugged. "Pretty much."

The key jingled in the lock at the front door and my parents walked in. The door swung back and bounced off of the wallpapered entryway. My mom's blonde hair was shorter than it had been last time they had been home and my dad's black hair had more gray sprinkled through it. They both rushed forward and wrapped their arms around me. The sink kicked on as Tracey washed her dishes and smiled at the *parent pile* I was in. They were both wearing matching sweatsuits. *Oh my gosh.* This is what I didn't miss at all. I almost expected a teacup pooch to prance in behind them, matching outfit and all. Thankfully, my inner prayers were answered when no dog was to be seen or smelled nearby.

Tracey grinned. "I love the matching outfits." Leave it to her.

I wanted to tell her not to encourage it but I was being squeezed too tightly to get the words out. My mom finally untangled herself from my side and rushed to Tracey. She wrapped her arms around my friend and closed her eyes like Tracey was her long lost daughter. "Thank you so much for being here for our baby girl."

Dad finally let go and I muttered, "Not a baby."

"What have you two been up to?" My mom eyed my half-eaten rare steak like she couldn't believe what she was seeing. She wasn't the only one. I hardly believed it too. I couldn't wait to hear what Dad thought. His face wasn't as open as Mom's.

Tracey and I looked at each other and grinned. "Nothing really. Lots of studying for the finals coming up."

"That's a few months away," Dad said as I dumped the contents on my plate into the garbage.

Tracey leaned against the counter and her honey hair brushed over the side of her shoulder. "Can never be too prepared."

Mom patted her hand. "I never thought she would stop partying, I guess we have you to thank for that."

The smile slipped from my face. No, they had Rafe to thank for that. I was sure Tracey was thinking the same thing as her face mirrored my own. I popped my knuckles to get my thoughts on anything else. I didn't have the luxury to think of him as often as I did. I hated that he took up so much space in my head.

"Thank you for coming over tonight, Tracey, I'll walk you out."

"Nice seeing you both! Enjoy being back in town, Mr. and Mrs. Rivers!" Tracey said over her shoulder.

She leaned over and grabbed her backpack before she followed me to the door. I didn't say a word until we reached her car. "What do I do?"

Tracey started her car and leaned into her seat. "Act normal?"

"My parents are practically vegan. They never wanted to push the lifestyle onto me so I was pretty much vegetarian."

Tracey's nose wrinkled. "That explained you not finishing your dinner. If you feel like you need to shift or anything, call me immediately. I can run through the woods to get here."

Everything would be fine. I hoped.

CHAPTER 21
JADE RIVERS

Except everything wasn't fine. My skin constantly itched. Eating vegan food was a no-go. I swallowed down a few spoonfuls of Mom's interpretation of Vegan Curry a few nights later and barely made it to the bathroom to throw it all up. Nothing would settle in my stomach except for meat. So that night, around two a.m. with my stomach grumbling, I sent the text. The only call for help I would ever type out.

Tracey- *"Meet me at the Pack House."*

Me- *"I don't think this is a good idea."*

Tracey- *"I don't think you're that hungry."*

But it had been almost four days since I had been able to keep anything down. Pretending I was fine wasn't cutting it. My mom knew something was up. I was her baby, after all. Telling them I was still recovering wasn't going to cut it either.

After a few minutes and agonizing torture flooding my middle, I sent out a reply that I would be on my way. But how could I leave the house this late and not raise suspicion? I pressed my palms into my eyes. I needed to get an apartment or they needed to leave again but they wouldn't leave again until I was in tip-top shape. So I either had to get this curse under control or I needed to move out. Either way, I was in a tough spot. I didn't exactly have a job to move out, my parents had made sure I never wanted or needed for anything. If I told them I wanted to move out, there would be hell to pay and I wasn't ready for the argument or really the responsibility that would come with it all. How was I supposed to survive in the real world without them?

I crept down the hallway and froze when the light turned on in the living room. Dad sat in the recliner with his iPad on his lap. His feet were covered with black socks and propped up in front of him.

"What's up kiddo?"

I raised an eyebrow. "I could ask you the same thing."

He grinned. "I haven't been able to sleep lately."

I frowned. "Anything I can do to help?"

He shook his head and took his wire-framed

glasses from his face. "No, I don't believe so. Just the wolves again."

My body jerked. "Excuse me?"

"I have been having dreams about wolves lately so I figured I would stay up as late as I could to keep my brain from going into such a weird state in order to create the dreams. I'm trying to exhaust my subconscious."

I almost exhaled in relief. "Right, okay."

"Are you going somewhere?" His eyes zeroed in on my Vans in my hand and my purse in the other.

"I didn't want to wake you or Mom," I began. "But Tracey needed me."

Dad shook his head and chuckled again. "I knew there was more than just studying going on."

I bit my lip. "Maybe for her. I've been out of trouble for a few weeks now." I tried to keep the grimace from my face at the memory of Rafe shoving the syringe into me. I didn't need to be reminded of the buzzkill he was.

"Well, you're a good friend for going to bail her out. I'll let your mom know that you'll be staying at her house tonight."

A foreign feeling washed through me. They had always been so chill, I didn't know what had worried me so much. Maybe it was partly the fact that I had never hidden anything from them before and here I was, hiding everything. I padded across the floor and leaned over to kiss my father on the cheek. He smiled against my lips and ruffled my hair.

"Be careful, make good choices,"

The drive to the Crimson Pack territory was short and it made me nervous. Would Rafe be there? Could I avoid him? Where the hell was I going to be sleeping because I knew Tracey didn't have much room at her parents' place. And her dorm was off-limits because there was no room for another person. I thought of my spacious backseat and nodded to myself. If it could hold two people hooking up, it could certainly hold me, alone, for one night. I'd borrow a blanket from Tracey or something.

The long winding driveway brought me a little peace and comfort. I still hadn't been able to shift and it left me with growing anxiety in my chest. Not that the entire situation didn't make me a raging lunatic to begin with, but that was another thing entirely. For the most part, I had accepted what was happening, like it was second puberty. The other parts of me just didn't want to adult or care or do anything. My knuckles turned white as I gripped the steering wheel with all of my strength or what I imagined all of my strength could be. Tracey still had a lot to teach me and go over. All of the homes had their lights out except the main house.

Crimson Manor.

The Crimson Keep.

Hell itself.

I could have gone on and on in my head with all the silly nicknames but then there was Tracey grinning at me from the other side of the car and I had to stop. She probably wouldn't have liked all the disrespect for her pack to begin with.

I closed my fingers around the handle on my door and shoved it open. Tracey grinned. "Come on, we have food inside."

Hesitation held me tightly. "It's late, I'm sure everyone is sleeping. I thought we would swing by a fast-food place and get burgers or something."

Tracey's eyebrow hit her hairline as she regarded me. "I don't think you mean that. You want a greasy, long-dead animal over something a bit fresher with blood and not fat?"

My mouth salivated. "I don't want to wake anyone up."

Rafe's voice boomed across the porch. "I can

promise you that we are all awake. Your old fan belt made sure of that."

I swallowed back my retort as Tracey gave me a warning look and she replied, "Don't be an ass Rafe, everyone is out running as a pack or back here cooking for when the pack returns."

That made me feel better, slightly. Rafe scoffed. "We are feeding food to the outsiders now."

If I bit my tongue any harder I would have tasted blood, so I stopped and grinned. Except my grin was anything but friendly. "I wouldn't be here at all if it wasn't for you."

Rafe's eyes flashed before he turned on his heel. "You're right, you'd be dead." And he left it at that. What the hell was that supposed to mean?

Tracey's lips pressed together and she shook her head. "I don't know what that means. He doesn't tell my father much and he won't open up to anyone anymore. We fear a sickness is settling in because he hasn't found his mate yet."

That word just kept popping up in normal conversation around here. "You haven't picked a mate yet?" I found myself asking her.

Tracey bit the inside of her lip as I followed her into the pack house. The smell of steak hit me right in the face and I could have rolled over and shown my tummy for it. This was getting ridiculous. I rubbed my hands down my arms to get rid of the chill setting into my bare skin.

"Mates are complicated, especially when you're an Alpha." Tracey didn't bother with lowering her voice as we walked into the massive home. "The Alpha has a responsibility to the pack to find a mate soon after he becomes an alpha. If he doesn't he will get sick and risk the rest of the pack. My father is worried about him." She threw a daring look at Rafe as we took seats at the long dining table I had sat at a few days before.

"Now we tell the pack all of our secrets?" Rafe hummed before he crossed his massive arms over his chest. Much to my horror, my eyes followed the vascular veins bulging in his biceps. The biceps that were covered in tattoos. "Like what you see, stranger?"

I rolled my eyes. "I don't know how we could possibly be strangers after what you did to me."

"Is there something that needs to be discussed?" a woman asked from the doorway. Her hair was up in a beige towel and a robe was wrapped around her body. I knew immediately she was Rafe's mother. My mouth went dry.

Rafe wasted zero time. "I changed Jade against

her will."

Rafe's mother looked between the two of us as her dark eyebrows pulled together. "You better have a good reason for this, Rafe. You've been acting crazed lately."

Tracey threw me an *I told you so* look from across the table. I rolled my eyes. I didn't care if he was losing his sanity or not, that didn't give him a pass to hurt other people. I had the rest of my life to think about and he had ruined it all.

"You ruined my life," The words slipped past my lips before I could stop them. Rafe's glowing eyes snagged mine.

"I saved your life,"

"You're narcissistic," I bit out.

"One day you'll understand." He growled back.

Rafe's mother blinked. "I can't handle this. I don't know why you did what you did, but you have to make it right."

Rafe grinned with all of his teeth. He looked even more like a psycho. "She's not a part of our pack, I don't have to do shit."

There was a gasp as Rafe's mother slapped his cheek. "You are a lot of things, but first and foremost, you are the Alpha to this pack. If you don't start acting like it, I'll challenge you myself."

CHAPTER 22
JADE RIVERS

I knew I should have questioned sleeping arrangements sooner but as it grew later and later, I knew my options were limited. Low and behold, I ended up sleeping at the Crimson Manor.

Alice Crimson, Rafe's mother, walked me up the stairs to my room while Tracey shot me apologetic looks from the side of the stairs. I rolled my eyes. This was just my luck. Alice sighed as we made it to the top of the stairs before she turned to look back at me.

"I know my son seems a bit irrational but I do believe it's the mating call leading him to act this way." She continued to the first door on the left and pushed it open. "I also know that if you don't join a pack, your wolf will kill you."

I pressed my lips together. Great. Tracey had

mysteriously left that one out. I was damned if I did and I was damned if I didn't. "Maybe I would be okay with that."

Alice turned to me and shook her head. "No, you wouldn't be. I see the fight in you. I know you wouldn't be okay with that at all. I'm not telling you to swear under Rafe. God no, especially with all the trauma he has put you through, but you'll have to move to find another pack and you might not make it in time."

I thanked her for her words of wisdom and closed the door behind me. The room smelled like pine and something sweeter, like cinnamon rolls. I closed my eyes and inhaled deeply. This wasn't so bad. Rafe had disappeared after he had made sure everyone in the pack ate and I knew I wouldn't see him in the morning.

Tracey had insisted that pack duties happened on the weekend, whatever that meant and I could explore some more of the Crimson land. I didn't know if I felt comfortable doing that just yet, but it was something to keep my mind occupied.

🐾

By six am the entire pack house was buzzing with movement and whispers. I could hear people talking as they woke up or as they slipped in and out of the house. I was still eating the concoction Tracey's grandmother had given me, but little by little it wasn't working as well. I still didn't need my contacts which was a relief, but eventually my parents would notice that. They made sure I took care of my eyes, my eyesight had been the worst since I was little. They were anal about me eating the right foods to help it improve too. What was I going to tell them? The carrots must have healed my eyes?

I yawned as a door slammed below and the force of it vibrated the floors. I knew it was Rafe. No one else seemed to have a temper like him except for Axel, Tracey's dad.

A knock on the door pulled me from my thoughts. "Yes?"

Tracey pushed the door open and leaned against the doorframe. She was still wearing her pajamas and her pant legs were tucked into some floral rubber boots. She was a style icon for sure.

"Saturdays don't mean sleeping in around here, sorry about that." I shrugged. Even though I was still groggy, my wolf or whatever it was didn't allow me to sleep in anymore. The itching in my chest always woke me up early. I rubbed in between my breasts to try to get the sensation to pass.

"What's the plan for today?" I asked as I pushed the blankets away from my legs.

"I would love to give you the tour of the property and tell you all about your alter ego hiding inside of you." Tracey grinned and I couldn't help but want to know more. This was the rest of my life, right? I couldn't just ignore the wolf side of me and eventually I was going to have to shift. I just didn't want to do it now.

She placed a bag at the foot of my bed and I smiled. I had forgotten I had packed a bag the night before. I had told my dad I was spending the night, being prepared to do so was on the agenda but I had also planned on sleeping in my car.

CHAPTER 23
RAFE CRIMSON

Axel kept his pace with me as we went around the perimeter again. The rogue wolves were getting close again. Their scent covered the property line. They were trying to mess with my head and it was working. Axel sighed as he crossed his arms over his chest.

"This must be stopped," Axel shook his head and gave me a worried glance.

"What do you think I should do about it?" I had never seen my father deal with rogue wolves growing up. Every single wolf in the pack was loyal to him even if they didn't like the decisions he sometimes made.

After I challenged my father when the sickness had become too much for him and won, some of the wolves didn't like it. They took their entire families and left. I had reached out to neighboring packs to see about their safe arrival but they never showed up. They never seemed to go anywhere. Their scents had been all but forgotten, until a few weeks ago when one of the rogue wolves had shown up at the party I was at. The party Jade was also attending. Neck tattoo guy. He had claimed I wasn't the true Alpha and challenged me, upstairs in front of humans.

It hadn't ended well for him or the rest of his friends that had attacked me afterward. But I was protecting myself and the damage had been burned away. Only a small bit of sprayed blood had been found and thankfully, I had been able to write it off as teenagers with blood play kink If we had any vampires in our territory, it probably would have made the story a bit smoother but most of them had left this place years ago, before I became Alpha.

Axel chuckled. "You don't ever want my advice but now you do? You should have taken it when I told you to stay away from Jade the first time."

I shook my head. I wasn't going to talk about Jade, I didn't need counsel on her. I did what I had to to keep her alive and that was all that mattered. My wolf was happy and sated now that she was going to live. "That isn't what I wanted to discuss."

"You will need to talk to me about it eventually."

I sighed. "I need to know what I should do about the rogues. I don't think they are going to stop their perusal of this land."

"Unless they come onto our territory and challenge you or harm one of our own, there is nothing we can do about it. Pack Law is very strict on these kinds of things." Axel ran his hand down the length of a tree and took a deep breath.

"Sometimes I don't understand Pack Law."

Axel's eyes watched something in the tops of the trees before he patted my back. It reminded me of something my father had done when I was little. "Rogues go crazy and going after them off of pack lands could hurt humans, could expose us. The Pack Law will come for them."

The Pack Law, also known as the High Wolves. They made sure the packs stayed in line and abided by the laws that were put into place thousands of years ago. They were the police of the wolves. They enforced the laws that we sometimes couldn't or wouldn't. I hadn't heard about them actually enforcing laws for awhile. It had probably been a hundred years or more. I scratched the back of my neck and was about to reply when I smelled her.

Honeysuckle and cinnamon wrapped around

me. My wolf stood to attention as my fur swam across my skin. Axel narrowed his eyes at me. He could smell her too but his wolf wasn't reacting the same way. I shook the feeling off and built a wall around my wolf inside of my mind. It would make him crazy later but would keep me sane now. I didn't need my wolf getting in the way.

CHAPTER 24

Tracey led me deep into the woods behind her parent's cottage. She waved her hands around as she spoke. "You have noticed that you can do more, right? Like things your human body couldn't do?"

I shrugged. "I mean I guess. That potion stuff seems to not be working anymore and each day I discover something new about myself."

Tracey grinned. "Like what?" She was really enjoying this too much.

"Like this morning I could hear people's conversations through the walls. My sense of smell has improved a lot, not as much after I was first changed, but it's good. I don't need contacts anymore."

"Have you tried to run yet?" Her grin seemed to grow bigger. I didn't know how it was even possible.

I shook my head. "Not yet, I didn't think that would change unless I was in my wolf form."

All of a sudden she was beside me then she was gone, in a blink of an eye she was back. She had two popsicles in her hands. She handed me one while she continued to smile.

"Not as fast as vampires, but I haven't ever raced one, so in my head, I'm faster." She flicked her hair over her shoulder.

Vampires too? Of course. There had to be an entire world out there that I knew nothing about. I hadn't been apart of it until now. I rolled my eyes as I licked the cold dessert.

"Why don't you try it out?" Tracey cocked an eyebrow.

I shook my head. "I don't run."

"Your wolf will thank you for it." Tracey shrugged but I could see the worry on her face.

I chewed on my bottom lip. I didn't see the point. I hadn't tried to shift and all I wanted were these heightened senses to go away. The only good thing out of all of this was my eyesight had improved. I couldn't face the music just yet. For the most part, I didn't feel any different and I didn't know if it was because I hadn't accepted the part of me that was a wolf... or that my wolf didn't want to come out to play. Either way, I was glad I still felt like me for the most part.

The growling undertone in my voice had gone away and I felt more in control of my senses besides this morning.

Once we broke through the thick tree line I was speechless. There was a beautiful brick home front and center, then behind it, there was a tiny cottage that had smoke billowing up from its brick chimney. It looked like something from a storybook. I raised my eyebrows as Tracey and she grinned again.

"I can't tell you how nice it is to be able to tell someone about all of this," She bunched up her shoulders before she released a breath. "To not have to hide myself. I mean... I never wanted to hide any of myself from my friends but unfortunately, there aren't many girls in the pack my age... at least not ones that aren't falling all over our Alpha."

I winced as I finished off the dessert between my fingers. "So how hard did you try to fake jump out of my window?" If her speed was like she demonstrated, then there was no way she couldn't have jumped from my window and landed without injury.

Tracey giggled. "That was the absolute worst. I was hoping you would get hammered that night so all I had to do was run us past the security system and then throw you through the window."

I frowned. "Unfortunately, *your* Alpha had other plans that night."

Tracey grasped the top of my arm gently. "I promise you that I would have never allowed that to happen. I didn't know. I thought he was going to get to know you, not do what he did. I will live the rest of my life trying to make up for it."

Just as I was opening up my mouth to say something a little lady opened the front door to the hut and my words disappeared. She looked just like Tracey, but her skin was darker. She grinned at us and I instantly knew that was her grandmother that she had called the witch. There were hardly any wrinkles on her face and her hair was bright and shiny.

"Granny this is Jade Rivers," Tracey rushed across the lot separating them and kissed her grandmother on the cheek. I followed behind her slowly and held my hand out to the woman once I was in front of her. I didn't know how introductions went around here. Everything seemed so tense all the time but that could have something to do with the way I was *turned*. I didn't think anyone knew what to do when it came to me. Which I didn't mind, I liked the space. I wasn't a freak show.

Her youthful hand grabbed mine and yanked me to her. She wrapped her strong arms around my waist and about squeezed the life out of me with her hug. Yep, she was definitely a grandmother. For a moment I savored the feel of her arms around me. The scent of lavender and sandalwood clung to her skin. Until that moment I hadn't realized how much I would have loved to have a grandma. I untangled myself from her arms and hesitantly took a step away from her warm embrace.

"I'm Granny to everyone around here, but you can call me by my name if you would like," I shook my head. I didn't need to be any more of an outcast than I already was. She ushered me forward into her home and all sorts of scents enveloped me. First, it was the lavender and sandalwood, then it was pine that reminded me of Rafe. Then vanilla and honey. I pinched the bridge of my nose. I had never been anywhere besides the supermarket that had overwhelmed my senses like this. I closed my eyes and then the smells disappeared. I blinked in surprise.

Granny's hand rubbed my shoulder. "I forget what it's like to have new wolves around here. The little ones stay away from my hutch and I encourage them to keep their distance." She winked and I felt a smile stretch across my face. This one was probably the first real one since I had pulled onto the Crimson property.

Granny's little cottage was full of shelves. Every single wall either had books or little bottles lining every square inch. Even though there didn't seem to be any electricity, the rooms were bright with natural lighting and candles. The room we had walked into from the front door was massive. The fireplace was set to the right while the kitchen was on the opposite wall. There was no seating, not even a couch. There were tables overflowing with cauldrons, beaker bottles, and books. On the floor in front of the fireplace were two worn-out cushions and a small table in between them. Curled up under the table was a white cat. Its haunches raised when it noticed us.

Tracey shivered as it ran out of the room. "Granny insists on keeping the stupid cat even though she knows the wolves don't like them and they don't like us."

Granny was the ultimate rebel. She scoffed. "A witch needs her extra eyes. I don't have a wolf's extra instincts like the both of you, so I need Chalice to do what I can't. She always comes back with useful information."

My eyebrows pulled together. "You're not a wolf then?"

Granny laughed and shook her head. "Gods no. I mated with a wolf, which was quite the scandal back in the day."

I found myself smiling again. The wood floors beneath my feet creaked as I walked to the cushions in front of the fire. It wasn't winter yet and I expected the open fire to be uncomfortable against my skin, especially since I could no longer sleep under the blankets. The wolf inside of me made me a space heater. I couldn't seem to get comfortable anymore but this was fine, which was a surprise. I figured it had something to do with Granny being a witch. Nothing around here would be uncomfortable.

"What brought you two all the way out here?" Granny leaned against the hearth with her fist on her hip.

Tracey shrugged. She sat cross-legged on the cushion across from me. "I was showing Jade the property before she decides on whether or not she wants to swear her life to this pack."

She knew I didn't want to do that but I let her continue to talk while Chalice, the white cat darted back into the house. Granny frowned and picked her up by the scruff on the back of her neck as she passed. Granny's eyes glowed white as she stared at something we couldn't see.

"Thank you, Chalice," Granny muttered. "We have guests."

CHAPTER 25

Rafe Crimson

Visitors were always a great thing to have around, except now. With Jade Rivers still on the property, I knew I was doomed from the moment they arrived. They came without a warning and that was enough to make me feel defensive. Something wasn't right.

I met them halfway down the drive through the woods to the Crimson Manor. Their Alpha, Gamble, rolled the window down. The stench of weed rolled out of the jacked-up truck. I didn't know why he let his wolves participate in smoking. It stunk and did absolutely nothing to our psyche. Maybe if it could get us high it would be one thing but it didn't. It just smelled awful. I crossed my arms over my chest as I gritted my teeth.

Gamble jutted his chin up and a wolfish grin spread across his face. He hadn't shaved in the months since I had seen him last and his bright orange beard looked like a massive kitchen sponge on his chin. "Rafe, my man, what's happening?"

I raised an eyebrow as I exhaled. "I could ask you the same thing."

Gamble's face went serious. "We are here on business, though we would love to stay for pleasure."

Which meant they had new wolves that were looking for mates. I hated this, especially with Jade somewhere on the property. It had been almost a year since we had done a Mate Meet and I didn't like to think that now was a good time. But I also couldn't turn Gamble down either. It was the rules of the Pack Law. His wolves needed mates and if they thought one was here, I had to step aside. As long as they were cordial with the women, I couldn't do anything about the matter. The only problem was the fact that I *had* changed someone against their will and I didn't need the Pack Law to come after me for that. My pack knew better than to talk to the Bruiser Pack, but that didn't mean Jade wouldn't open her big mouth. She was going to bring a lot of trouble down on us if I didn't get to her fast.

I felt myself smile at Gamble even though it didn't meet my eyes. "Head to the Manor and I will get all the girls rounded up. Or we can talk first."

Gamble tossed what was left of his blunt out the window and it took everything in me to not rip him from his truck. "You got it, Alpha."

Behind him, several other lifted trucks waited. A growl rumbled through my chest before I could stop it. The Bruisers' numbers seemed to grow more every time I saw them. Something wasn't right.

CHAPTER 26

JADE RIVERS

"You would do best to not leave this cabin," Tracey eyes bright eyes found mine.

Granny smacked Tracey's hand with a wooden spoon and it was such a grandma thing to do that I couldn't help but smile. "You know that she can't do that."

"She isn't sworn into the pack. There isn't anything they can do." Tracey rubbed her tender hand.

Granny shook her head. "No, she is on pack lands so she will be forced to abide by the Pack Law."

"Pack Law?" I asked.

Tracey sighed. "Pack Law is what keeps the wolves in order. It's a bunch of laws that old men made up thousands of years ago and we must abide by them to this day or the High Wolves will come to execute us."

My eyebrows kissed my hairline at that. "No pressure."

Granny grabbed a book from the wall and sighed. "The Bruiser Pack is here to initiate the Mate Meet. All eligible female wolves are required to be ready to meet their future mate."

"And what if I don't want a mate?" I crossed my arms over my chest.

Tracey pressed her lips together. "That's for your wolf to decide."

Somehow I ended up at the Crimson Manor dressed up with Tracey. Her hair was pulled away from her face and she wore the same leggings from the night I had been turned, and a tight black onesie under it. We hadn't had enough time to get to the trunk of my car so I wore one of Tracey's outfits. It was a tight high waisted skirt and a crop top with a moon and sun on each breast.

I had to admit it looked good on me, but that didn't keep the scowl from my face as all the wolves slunk from their vehicles. A few of the men licked their lips as they appraised us like we were meat. Thankfully it wasn't just the women of this pack lined up like this, there were also the eligible bachelors too. Though the other pack didn't have nearly as many females as they did males.

There was apparently the sniff meet, which meant they had to sniff our necks. I was beyond grossed out and wished I could tuck tail and hide. But I knew that wasn't an option. I wasn't going to show weakness to these bastards. Especially Rafe. I could feel his eyes on me even though I refused to acknowledge him. Then he did the thing I absolutely didn't want him to do. He cut in front of one of the other pack members and pressed his nose to the hollow of my throat like he did the night he turned me.

My teeth mashed together so hard I was certain they would shatter. I placed my hands on either side of his shoulders and shoved him away from me. I hadn't expected it to work, he was so large but he stumbled backwards a few steps with a look of surprise on his face.

One of the men from the other pack barked out a laugh that boomed around me. "Oh, I like her. I like her a lot."

Rafe growled and I swore his eyes glowed. "I promise you that you don't."

The redhead took a step forward and everything inside of me screamed to run, not to submit, but to run. I worked the inside of my cheek between my teeth as he prowled closer to me. Rafe kept his distance but I could feel his anger in the air. He didn't want this man anywhere near me either. The big brute boxed me in against the house but didn't press his nose to my neck. He ran his hand down the back of my hair.

A growl rumbled through my chest, much louder than ever before. "If you touch me again, you will lose a hand."

"I'm Gamble, what's your name?"

I exhaled hard. "Not interested."

Gambles brown eyes flashed yellow before he narrowed them. He leaned in close as he whispered. "I like them wild, so I can break them."

My foot itched to kick him in the nuts. No man would ever speak to me that way. Tracey's hand on my wrist was the only thing that kept me docile. I didn't know much about this Pack Law but for now, I had to abide by it. Even if I really wanted to hurt the stupid brute in front of me.

Copper filled my mouth as my teeth dug into my

tongue. I grinned and knew that the bright red blood showed in my teeth. "Good luck breaking me, someone already tried that once and I think he's regretting it still."

Tracey snickered beside me and a growl rumbled across from me again. Without looking, I knew it was Rafe. Satisfaction rolled through me. Then Gamble took a step back and whistled low.

"I like her Rafe, how much to get her to change alliances?"

Rafe chuckled darkly and his eyes were glowing. "I doubt she would care how much money you have or offer her. She is... truly one of a kind."

This time I felt my teeth elongate. "Don't you forget it either, asshole."

I didn't specify who I was speaking to because it was to both of them. Were all Alphas douchebags? I would probably have to move very far away to find a man unlike these two.

I blinked at the way my thoughts had turned. Find a man? I didn't want or need a man but I would need an understanding and good Alpha to lead me, right? Or were they all this way?

Some of the members of the Crimson Pack walked off with ones from the Bruiser Pack and then

Tracey and I were left alone with the Alphas. Couldn't they just find their mates already?

"Is that all of your wolves?" Rafe finally asked Gamble.

Gamble ran his hand down his fluffy beard. "No, I have one that was running behind. Though I doubt he even cares about the Mate Meet."

Rafe nodded his head as he scowled. Something was bothering him. He was usually broody but there was a tense set to his shoulders. There was an awareness that he didn't usually have. Having this pack here was making him nervous.

My ears picked up a sound a few miles away and I blinked in surprise. Tracey's light eyes found mine as she shrugged. Maybe this was the late one that Gamble had been talking about. A Mustang rolled through the treeline at the end of the driveway. The entire vehicle was blacked out. I could practically feel myself salivating. I had thought Rafe had broken me from bad boys but as soon as the man stepped out of his car, my body broke out in chills.

Maybe I wasn't broken at all. The man that stepped out of the car wore a leather jacket over a white shirt and black ripped jeans covered thick legs. I swallowed hard as Tracey gripped my hand again. Both of our breathing had shallowed out as we watched the hottie stride across the parking lot. Nothing else moved as he did. I swore I wasn't even breathing when he stopped in front of Rafe and extended his hand. Tattoos covered every inch of his skin except his neck and his face. From here I could make out a few of the larger pieces. They were of wolves and the woods, but the smaller ones were harder to make out as he moved.

Tracey leaned in. "I don't know about you but I would love to explore all of those... *tattoos.*"

I grinned and nodded. "I am right there with you."

Tatts turned around and smiled at the both of us. The sunlight caught something in his eyebrow and Tracey gasped. "He's a turned wolf."

"What do you mean?" I leaned into her.

"His eyebrow piercing. It's next to impossible to get piercings if you're born a wolf."

"Hmm?" I raised my eyebrows.

"The skin heals too quickly."

"Then how does Rafe have tattoos?" I frowned. I had only gotten a little glimpse of his arms.

Tracey winced. "Wolves can get tattoos but only if there is wolfsbane in the ink. It's an extremely expensive, long, excruciating process. That's why it's usually the dominant wolves that have them. Lesser wolves don't have the willpower."

From what I could tell Gamble didn't have any tattoos. Tracey leaned in again and this time her voice was hardly audible. "Fake Alpha."

My eyes snapped to hers. Gamble was a fake Alpha? Was that possible? How did that come to be? Were others in on it?

The new man ran his tongue over his teeth as he approached us. "Good evening, ladies,"

Tracey hiccuped and I tried to keep myself from laughing at how ridiculous all of this was. Tracey squeezed my hand before letting go. "I think my grandmother needed my help in her herb garden."

I frowned at her and was about to reply when she disappeared. She had left me with Tatts. I rubbed my temples before I extended my hand to the newcomer. "I'm Jade, that was Tracey and her weird ass self."

His eyes didn't leave mine and warmth pooled low in my belly. I was definitely no longer immune to the bad boys. This was very bad but also not terrible. He accepted my outstretched hand and a smirk played on his lips. "Tracey the half-witch."

I raised my eyebrows. "I don't know if I would

call her that. Do you have a name, or should I just call you Tatts?"

He chuckled and once again warmth pooled in my abdomen. I had serious issues. "I'm Carden."

Even his name was hot. *Oh, help me.*

"Nice to meet you," Two growls sounded beside me as my voice got all breathy. My eyes flicked to Rafe's and I let out a growl myself. I wasn't going to be bullied by any asshole Alpha today, especially not with Carden in front of me. The last thing I wanted him to think was that I was weak.

"Have you ever been to a Mate Meet?" Carden put his hand on my lower back and guided me away from the new two Alpha-holes.

I took a deep breath. "Not exactly, I'm kind of new to all of this."

He chuckled and then his scent hit me. Rum, clove, and something citrus... like maybe, orange. A chill worked its way down my spine.

"Me too, I can smell that you were recently turned," He leaned forward and for a long agonizing minute, I waited for him to press his nose to my throat like Gamble had done. Instead, he pulled away from me and shoved his hands into his pockets.

Was that a good thing or a bad thing? "And what does that smell like?"

Carden cocked his head and gave me a face. "Like you haven't decided on something. Your scent is all over the place."

I didn't know what that meant but I knew it had something to do with Rafe. I looked over my shoulder ready to throw him a scowl but he was gone and so was the other Alpha. Carden looked up at the trees above us and my eyes followed the movement of his sharp jaw. I shrugged my shoulders. "Maybe I haven't decided anything yet."

He cocked an eyebrow as he brought his gaze back down to mine. "Oh? Like what?"

"My wolf hasn't exactly been corporative," Which wasn't exactly a lie but wasn't really the truth either. I hadn't really cared if she came around but now with Carden in the game, I felt like I needed my wolf to get her ass in gear. Which was silly. I had never fumbled like this over a man before. They usually came to me willingly and I decided whether they were worth my time after a few minutes. My body seemed to be telling me that Carden was definitely worth my time.

He leaned into me and I got the strong scent of citrus again. "Maybe we should let her out to play."

His eyes shifted from blue to yellow in a second and I felt panic well up in my chest. I wasn't ready to shift, especially not in front of this hot guy. Knowing me, I would make a complete fool of myself in the process.

I bit down on my bottom lip and shook my head hard. "No, that's okay. She's not really in the running mood."

Carden narrowed his eyes and took a step away from me. "So, what do you like to do for fun around these parts? Our Pack isn't anywhere near a college campus, I would imagine it gets rather crazy around here."

I licked my lips, thankful for the change in conversation. "Yes, there are ragers almost every night."

A smile played on his lips and he ran his hand through his blonde hair. "I would love to go to one of these parties with you, if you're up for it."

It was the weekend and I could easily tell my parents I was going on a date. Which would make them ecstatic. I hadn't been on a date in what seemed like forever. I ran my hands down the front of my borrowed skirt. "I would like that very much. Why don't you put your number in my phone and

I'll send you my address for you to pick me up later?"

Carden cocked his head to the side. "Like a date?"

I couldn't tell if he was happy with that or not. But I also didn't care. If he wanted to go to one of these parties with me, he would be my date. I wasn't going to end up at another party alone and in danger.

CHAPTER 27

My mom was the one waiting for me when I got home. Before I had left the Crimson Pack's property I had made sure to change into my clothes again and speak to Tracey. She had met one of the wolves from the Bruiser Pack after he had gotten bored with one of the other girls. So somehow, it had turned into a double date, which I didn't mind but I didn't know how Carden would feel about it.

"How was Tracey last night?" my mom asked from the kitchen as the front door closed behind me.

"She was good, just a little drunk and needed a ride home." Which was a complete lie because were-wolves couldn't get drunk unless there was wolfs-bane in the alcohol. I had come to discover this as I was changing back into my clothes before I left pack lands. Tracey tucked a flask of it in my center console and grinned. Apparently, this was also expensive and if Rafe found out I had it, we would both be in big trouble. Which only made me want it more. Anything to get under his skin and bother him as much as he did me.

"I'm glad that you have a friend and can be a good friend to her," Mom said with her back to me as she pulled something from the oven. From the smell of it, I knew it was roasted tofu. My stomach lurked. My mom's roasted tofu was the best, but my wolf didn't like the smell of it at all. I would have to fake it for her benefit or she would know something was wrong with me.

"What does that mean?" I leaned onto the island and went to pick at the top of the tofu. She swatted my hand away just like she always did. I smiled. I was going to have to really fake this good.

"You have always been so worried about the escape that you never got close to anyone."

I blinked at her. She had never tried to get deep with me and she had never really spoken with me on my friendships before. Why was she calling me out on this now?

"Escape?" I took a bottle of water out of the fridge and tried to ignore the icy pain in my chest from her words.

"I didn't ever think you were depressed but maybe, we should have gotten you evaluated before." Dark circles surrounded my mother's eyes.

"I'm not depressed," *I'm lonely.* But I couldn't bring myself to say it. I couldn't bring myself to hurt her in that way. I was lonely because I wanted to be alone but I also didn't. I had never tried to get close to anyone because I had never seen it done before. I had no example of how to be a friend. So for one night a week, I escaped to the parties to make myself feel whole. To make myself feel like I wasn't so lonely.

I thought of Tracey then and I wondered if I would still feel so alone if I hadn't been turned. Would she still be close with me? Or would she have eventually left too? For once since Rafe had turned me, I didn't feel like I needed to party, but tonight I wanted to. For once I didn't feel so alone and hollow. I felt like I belonged to something besides a party and school.

"Then what is going on?" She sighed. "You have thrown yourself into school work lately, so maybe it isn't as bad or maybe that's worse."

I grabbed her hand and pulled her in for a hug. She was a worrier. A worrier for no reason some-times and this time, I could see that it was weighing heavily on her shoulders. She took a deep breath and pressed a kiss to the top of my head. "I think I'm just trying to figure out who I am."

Mom let out a shuddering breath before we released each other and she went back to the stove to prepare something to go with her tofu. "We really like Tracey and hope she stays around."

I pressed my lips together into a smile and sighed. I hoped so too.

I toned my usually risqué look down for the night, knowing that my father would have a heart attack if I came down the stairs in my usual party wear. It was starting to get a tad cooler outside and even though I could no longer feel it like I could before, I had to pretend for the sake of my parents. How could I break the news that I had been turned into a werewolf? I still wasn't certain that it had happened to me yet. I probably had a slight case of denial. I would imagine it would go away as soon as I saw my wolf for the first time. And who knew when that would happen? I wasn't about to hold my breath.

Dark wash jeans and a *thin* black sweater. My Converse squeaked as I rushed down the stairs. He told me he would come to the door to get me but I knew as soon as my parents saw the tattoos and the piercing... I was a goner. He was waiting in his blacked-out car at the road. My dad was back in his recliner with his laptop on the side table. My mom was finishing up their dinner when I grabbed my purse and keys.

"Wait, where are you headed?" Mom called from the kitchen. "Roasted tofu is your favorite!"

I grimaced. "I didn't know you were making it tonight or I possibly wouldn't have accepted a date."

My dad sat up in his chair and put his reading glasses on top of his computer. "A date?"

"A date?" My mom repeated from the kitchen.

I took a deep breath. "Yep and I'll be late if we continue this conversation!"

Before my dad could get up from his chair and my mom could turn the corner, I was out of the door and rushing down the driveway at a much faster pace than I was used to. Just as I got near Carden's Mustang, he rushed from his side of the car in were-wolf speed to open my door for me. My heart stopped.

"If you won't let me come to your door, then you will at least let me open this one for you." His voice was like caramel on my insides.

All I could manage was a quick nod. I slipped into his car and found myself surprised. It wasn't junked out like all the one night stand's cars had been. It was clean and shiny.

"You didn't have to go through all the trouble of cleaning just for me," I joked.

Carden got behind the wheel and leveled me with his steely gaze. "If you paid as much as I did for this car, you would keep it clean too."

I raised my eyebrows. "Touché."

CHAPTER 28

RAFE CRIMSON

Rage was a new feeling for me. I was used to being angry. Most of the time I was angry but as I watched Carden open Jade's door for her, I felt something new rip through my chest. The only good thing about the situation was that she had kept her clothes conservative tonight. I wouldn't have been to blame if she had worn what she did the night *I* turned her.

When I had overheard their conversation in the woods about her being turned recently, I wanted to march over there and make sure the entire property heard that I was the one that did it. But doing that would only make things more difficult on my wolf and Jade's. Carden was right, Jade's scent was all over the place. Her wolf didn't know what to do and my presence wasn't making things any easier. I saw the angry glances she shot my way each time we were around each other.

As much as I wanted to stay away and not interfere... I knew one thing. I was going to that party tonight, consequences be damned.

CHAPTER 29
JADE RIVERS

Experiencing a party now was completely different. The music thrummed through my veins as we neared the frat house. I had expected to feel some kind of pain or PTSD because of what had happened the last time I had been at a party. The night Rafe had turned me but I felt nothing. There was no bitterness in my mouth or even a touch of panic. There was something new, a new feeling of excitement. I had never gone to a party with someone before. The thought of walking into that frat house without having to look for anyone was a new sensation. I liked it.

Carden peeked over at me and grinned. His white teeth were a tad sharp and they reminded me of the predator that was hiding beneath his skin -our skin. "You ready?"

He held his hand out to me. "Never been readier."

I held his hand for a moment before he zoomed out of the car, around to my door. He leaned against my open door with a sly look. "Having that kind of speed never gets old."

I narrowed my eyes at him as I looked around his vehicle. I was still too new to all of this. "Aren't you afraid someone will see you?"

He rolled his eyes. "Not really. Mostly everyone is drunk here. What are they gonna do?"

I ran my tongue over the front of my teeth and nodded my head. He did have a point. He grabbed my hand again but this time there was no smile on his face. He narrowed his eyes at the people milling around us. It was still early, though most everyone had started drinking hours before. The proof of it was on the front balcony of the home. A few passed out bodies already.

Carden's shoulders were squared off and tense. He was worried about something. I yanked him to a stop and he sighed. "I have never felt so out of control with my powers before. The music makes it feel funny. The pulsing sounds are muffling the rest of my senses and it's making it hard for me to concentrate."

I pressed my lips together in worry. "We don't have to stay."

I wasn't feeling the same things as him but it could have been because of a number of things. Starting with the part that I had only shifted once and I couldn't feel my wolf prowling under my skin.

Carden gave me a pained grin. "No, I want to stay. I would hate for you to waste looking that good."

I couldn't help the retort that passed my lips. "Too bad my parents are home and you don't get to see how I *really* dress."

Tracey confirmed it as she walked up the driveway behind us. "Did you just get out of church?"

She was wearing a tight dress that laced up her chest. There was no way she could wear any underwear with that on. Her full breasts were on display tonight and I raised my eyebrows at her in question. She was usually more reserved.

"Where is your date?"

Tracey waved her hand behind her. "He's parking the car."

A few minutes later the breath left my lungs when Tracey's date walked up the lawn and looped his arm through my friend's. This wasn't right. She told me she had a date, but why hadn't she mentioned it was Rafe?

He grinned and it didn't meet his eyes. "You look *nice* tonight, Jade."

I felt my lip lift up in a snarl. "Everything would be nicer if you weren't here."

Rafe cocked his head. "I doubt that. I wish you would have worn that leopard print crop top and those leather leggings in your dresser."

Not only had he been in my room, but he had also gone through my drawers. I let out a slow snarl. "You're a panty thief and a creep, I wonder what else will be added to your resume tonight."

Rafe let out a bark of a laugh while Tracey did nothing to hide her mortification of the situation, all while Carden looked between the three of us like we were insane. We probably were. I grabbed his hand in mine and marched away from my *friend* and my enemy.

It wasn't until we were inside that Carden stopped me and I pulled the flask from my clutch. I took a long burning swig before I gave it to him. His fingers brushed mine as he took it and his lips turned down into a frown. He took a long chug before he tucked it back into my bag. "Wolfsbane is the nastiest shit."

I shrugged. "Do you want to get drunk or watch the drunks?"

His lips stretched across his teeth in amusement. "I suppose I would like to get drunk. It has been a long time since I tried. Wolfsbane is too expensive for our pack."

The music thumped around us and shook the walls but I had no trouble hearing my date over it. He still grabbed my waist and yanked me to him. I didn't know if it was the music or the Wolfsbane in the works but I didn't mind one bit. It had been too long since I had male attention like *this*.

The flask was empty within an hour and I could feel the effects of it lulling me into a comfortable stupor. Rafe and Tracey were nowhere to be seen and I honestly didn't care. I felt betrayed that she hadn't even warned me. Just as I was starting to taste anger in my mouth, Carden grabbed my hands in his and yanked me to the middle of the living room. The floors were spotted with different kinds of drying liquids and there was a slight scent of vomit in the air. But for a moment, I felt like I was normal again. Like I wasn't turned and I didn't have to worry about animal instincts or stupid alphas. For once I felt like I was me again and that was all that mattered.

Carden kept his hands on my waist while we

bumped and ground to the music. My eyes slowly fell closed as he pulled me closer to him. Sweat dotted my brow but I didn't dare stop. It felt too good to be pressed against his warmth. His scent wrapped around me and drowned out the sweat of the other bodies around me. A hum worked its way up my throat and I felt a rumble of approval at my back.

Carden's arms tightened around me and my mouth went dry. The effects of the Wolfsbane were starting to wear off but that was the last thing I was worried about. A delicious heat had started to tug at my lower belly and the last thing I was worried about was whether or not I was going to leave this party drunk. The only thing that I was worried about was leaving the party with him.

A gentle touch on my arm had my eyes snapping open. My body stopped its gyrating, even as Carden continued to pull on me and rub on me. The pooling in my stomach hadn't stopped but it wasn't as strong as I stared into the yellow eyes of my friend.

I frowned. "What is it?"

She swallowed hard and shook her head.

I pressed her. She wasn't going to interrupt this if it wasn't important. Her hair was a wild mess around her head and for a minute, a little one, I wondered if she had gone another level with Rafe. If they had left the friend territory she promised they were hardly in.

"Can I talk to you?" I looked over my shoulder to ask Carden if he was ready to go but Tracey's hand on mine had me looking back at her. "Alone?"

I blinked through the lusty haze that had wrapped around me and told Carden I would be right back. He left the dance floor with us but leaned against the wall in the kitchen as Tracey yanked me out into the backyard, where a dying garden awaited us.

"I don't think this double date was such a good idea," Tracey muttered as she ran her hands down her face.

I ground my teeth together. "Did Rafe hurt you? Are you okay?"

Tracey's head snapped up and her mouth went into an O shape. "No, never. He would never do anything like that. I agreed to be his date tonight because he was going to come alone. I figured it would be better to keep my eyes on him."

I nodded my head. "Okay, so what's wrong?"

"Do you feel anything with Carden?" I blinked at her.

"What do you mean?" I asked.

"Like do you feel a connection with him or a mate's pull?"

My eyebrows pushed together as I shook my head. "I don't think so, but I am insanely attracted to him."

"I just think if you aren't feeling a mate's pull, then maybe you should tread carefully."

It hit me then, why Rafe was here. "Did Rafe put you up to this?"

Tracey bit her lip. I had never seen her so nervous before. "No, but he's not doing very good tonight and I don't know what to do."

"Then maybe he needs to leave." I shrugged my shoulders. I hated to cut the party short for her, but I wasn't the one that brought the deranged wolf as my date.

Tracey's eyes flicked to something behind me and my back went straight. I wasn't going to back down on this. Slowly, ever so slowly, my arms crossed over my chest. Tracey shook her head. "This isn't going to end well, I think I need to call someone to bring some more spiked booze." She laughed nervously but I didn't know what to do. I couldn't let Rafe continue to ruin my life. I had to live and I was going to do whatever it took to do so.

CHAPTER 30

It had been hours since I had seen Tracey and her extra spiked booze. We hadn't gone through it quickly this time. Carden had a flask in his pocket and I had one in my bag. We took turns sipping on it slowly, savoring the nasty burn it created down our throats.

This time we weren't dancing, which was fine, I didn't really care about that too much. I just wanted to be. I wanted to feel like I had before I had been turned. I wanted to feel normal again, even if this wasn't normal at all. I could try.

So when Carden's arm wrapped around my shoulders, I let myself feel the excitement. When his fingers rubbed lazy circles over my collarbone, warmth pooled deep within my belly. When his lips found the shell of my ear, my body went liquid. A deep sigh escaped me.

His whisper sent shivers down my back. "Why don't we get out of here."

My breath hitched in my throat and I nodded as he wrapped his fingers around mine. He pulled me through the throngs of people that had only gotten thicker as the minutes had passed. When we broke through the threshold, the night air was crisper than it had been before and it caused my skin to pebble with the chill. When we made it to the lawn Carden stopped in his tracks. I was about to ask him what was wrong when he whipped around, and yanked me toward him. His hand found the hollow of my throat and shoulder. His eyes looked like liquid honey as he gazed down at my eyes then my lips. The corners of his mouth picked up slightly.

"I've been thinking about doing this all night," and then his lips were on mine and I couldn't think straight. Whether it was the physical contact and my heightened senses or the spiked booze, I didn't know. But my body melted all the same. A growl rumbled through Carden's chest and I shivered in response. His lips moved against mine and it was torture. It had never felt like this before. His mouth tasted like rum, wolfsbane, and that citrus undertone again. His tongue slid against the seam of my lips and I didn't know why we had started this in front of the frat house but I needed this to be in the car, anywhere but here. Where I felt the eyes of someone or multiple people watching. Not that it mattered, there were worse things happening inside but the last thing I wanted was to give a show. Maybe once upon a time I would have been interested in such a thing, but not today, not now. Not with my wolf so out of my grasp I never knew what would happen next.

He parted my lips with his own and I could feel the hunger growing within me. I couldn't control it but I pulled away all the same. Carden's lips were red and swollen, his eyes were now bright yellow. I would have to ask Tracey about that later. His hand reached up and he ran rough fingers down my cheek before he grabbed my hand again and pulled me to his car.

My heart raced and my body felt light and airy. I touched my lips with my free hand, they were just as swollen and sensitive as Carden's looked to be. The usual nerves or awkwardness that hit me when we got to the car didn't happen this time. It was a smooth, comfortable silence. One that I wasn't prepared for as the door clicked closed and we were zooming away from the party. I didn't feel like it had only been a few hours, at least that was what the clock said on the dash. We hadn't been there very long but I didn't care anymore. Especially when his hand slipped over my leg and gripped my thigh. Delicious heat washed over me again. I had to fight myself to keep my eyes open. But through the lust-filled haze on my brain, I remembered Tracey. My back straightened as I peered over my shoulder at the frat house fading.

"I forgot to tell Tracey we were leaving," I muttered sadly. I hadn't meant to leave without her but I had completely forgotten about her since we had started slowly sipping on the spiked booze. My heart sank slightly. I had told myself I had wanted to be a better friend, but this was not that. I wasn't being a good friend to her at all. I had left her with the psycho. My shoulders slumped.

Carden squeezed my leg. "She left hours ago,"

I frowned. That didn't sound right, that didn't sound like Tracey but maybe she had brought Rafe home. I had encouraged her to do that. Did she really listen?

Carden squeezed my leg again and I was brought back to the present and away from my thoughts. "Maybe she wanted you to enjoy your night if she wasn't going to."

He had a point. My lips pulled into a small smile as his grip tightened on my leg. I didn't recognize where we were headed and a part of me was slightly worried. The girl that I had been before I was turned would have been terrified. But this girl didn't feel that way. I knew that I could hold my own more than I could have before. I knew that I could kill with my bare hands if I needed to, not that I wanted to. But desperate times called for desperate measures. So I let myself relax because I deserved to have a good time tonight and find someone that would take care of me. Mind. Body. Soul. I didn't know if Carden was that person but I was about to figure out if he could take care of my body, that was for sure. He turned down the road that led to the children's park on the other side of town and I had to bite my lip to keep myself from smiling. I had heard of people coming here to *park* but had never experienced it myself. It was dark, zero street lights, and woods surrounded it. I wondered if he had chosen it for that reason for his wolf or because there was no one else here. His windows were blacked out enough that it really didn't matter if there was an entire parking lot full but I liked that we were alone. My ears were starting to become sensitive again. A squirrel was running through the trees above us. If there had been people around, it would have been a mood killer.

He pulled into a parking spot that faced the woods and flicked the headlights off. When he leaned across the center console I was putty. All rational thought flew straight out the window. I leaned into him and when our lips met that hunger ramped up inside of me. My hands went to his neck and his grip on my leg shifted to my waist. All while our lips explored each other and my heart pounded in my chest. My fingers trembled slightly as I dragged them down the front of his shirt then grabbed either side of his jacket. My lips didn't leave his as he shrugged the clothing off. His tongue slid along my lips again and this time I opened up for him.

The taste of Carden exploded in my mouth and a growl rumbled through my chest this time. Carden pulled away and I opened my eyes to find him surprised. His eyes weren't as yellow as they had been before. When he grinned it was completely wolfish. All rational thought left my head again as I launched myself at him. We were a tangle of hands, claws?, and pants of air.

He shoved me back into my seat and climbed over the center console. Everything inside of me stopped working as he knelt in front of me and looked into my eyes. I didn't know how either of us even fit like this but no rational thought or logic could come into play now. He leaned over me and my heart skipped a beat. His hands grasped my waist and I didn't know if I was even breathing anymore. One of the hottest men was *kneeling* in front of me. This was dangerous but I liked it. No, I craved it. Dangerous men like this kneeling was something I didn't know I wanted. Didn't know I *needed*.

My head tilted back to give him better access as his lips grazed my neck. A breathy sigh escaped my lips and Carden gave me a growl of approval. How I knew it was approval was beyond me, I could hardly think straight but it was like my wolf knew.

But when his teeth grazed my neck, my wolf didn't like it. I could instantly tell. My back straightened and my heart pounded in my chest. I knew Carden could hear it. I tried to angle away from him but he didn't care. His body was now pinning mine down and then his teeth did it again, right in the hollow of my throat. The place Rafe had sniffed. This wasn't right, something was wrong. A whimper escaped my lips and the wolf inside of me felt like she shrunk away. I wanted to scream at her to not leave me, I needed her. I needed her strength.

Carden's body shifted and his teeth became sharper on my neck. This wasn't right. All desire was gone now.

"Carden," I gasped as I tried to angle my neck away from his sharp teeth. He didn't stop. Panic flared inside of my chest. This had to stop. I pressed my hands into his chest and pushed. He only leaned into me more. "Carden, please, something isn't right."

He snarled inside and when his eyes peeked up at me they were bright yellow. They were the brightest I had ever seen them or anyone else's. I swallowed and shook my head against the seat.

I am strong. I am a she-wolf. I can do the hard things. I won't let this wolf get the best of me. I repeated this over and over in my head as I tried to push his body off of mine. His body was a lot stronger than mine. I pressed my hands into his chest again.

"I don't want to do this Carden, I don't think I'm ready." My voice shook but I was determined. I wasn't going to let whatever he was doing happen. He wasn't going to put his teeth on me. It was *wrong*. My wolf hated it. I hated it. But more than those things, I hated that he wasn't listening.

His teeth latched onto my neck and fight lifted my limbs. Whatever he had planned wasn't going to continue. I punched and kicked, every single blow hit him but he didn't move. His teeth just continued to press into the sensitive skin on my neck and I knew that no matter how hard I fought, I was going to lose. Nausea rolled through me.

One minute Carden's teeth were pressed into my neck and then the next there was a rush of cold air as the car door was ripped open and then Carden's body was off of mine. I breathed a sigh of relief. Maybe his wolf had gotten out of control and he didn't know what to do. I hadn't asked Tracey about that. She said that sometimes the wolf side of them- us- got out of control and there was little they could do to stop it. I took a deep breath and then I realized that Carden hadn't gotten back in the car and that my door was still open and the cold air was hitting me.

My breath left me as I opened my eyes. The door hadn't been opened, it had been ripped off. I swallowed hard and pressed my trembling hands into my lap. Had Carden done that?

A growl sounded on the other side of the car and I knew immediately that it wasn't Carden that had done that to his car. It wasn't Carden that had willingly removed himself from me. Something wet trickled down the side of my neck and I pressed my fingers into it. All at once, my senses snapped back to me like a rubber band popping.

The scent of copper was heavy in the air and I didn't know if it was from my bleeding neck or something else. There was a tugging within my chest and for a moment, I knew it was my wolf perking up at the sounds around us.

A little late there. I wanted to scold her.

The growling grew louder and then there was a snapping of teeth. I peeled myself from the wrecked vehicle and approached the sounds. My eyes adjusted to the darkness immediately and I saw it. Two wolves circling each other on the other side of Carden's mustang. One was a blur of midnight fur and the other was the color of sand. I immediately knew who the sandy-colored one was but the midnight wolf was one I couldn't figure out. Had he heard my pleas for help from the woods and came to investigate?

My fingers stayed on my bleeding neck while the midnight wolf circled Carden's wolf. They both let out menacing growls at each other before the black wolf's eyes met mine. They were blood red.

Crimson.

CHAPTER 31

JADE RIVERS

A silver Volvo's headlights appeared down the street and the panic I had been feeling in the car amped up. A human couldn't see what was happening here. I had to distract them. I had to do something. Maybe I could call Tracey. I had to call Tracey. I gazed down at the wrecked vehicle and quickly extracted my purse from the passenger seat. I rushed to the car as it grew closer and it slammed into park. I looked into the wild eyes of my best friend behind the wheel. Relief crushed my chest and my knees wobbled.

I wrapped my arms around myself to keep the shaking from starting. What was with these wolves? Why did they have to keep ruining the fun I was trying to have? A life I was trying to live? Couldn't I have a normal life? What did fate have against me?

Tracey's door swung open and before I could blink she had her arms wrapped around me. Then she threw her head back and pushed me at arm's length to inspect the bite on my neck. She breathed out a sigh of relief before she yanked me back into her arms.

"How did you know?" I found myself saying into her hair.

She stiffened. "I'm not sure if you're ready for that conversation."

I looked over at the two wolves fighting and I believed her. I didn't want to know right now because I knew it was going to make me angry enough to get in between the two monsters hashing it out.

My body was still trembling when we pulled into the Crimson Pack's lands. The Bruiser Pack's vehicles and trucks were still parked everywhere but I couldn't hear the chatter of their conversations. I chalked it up to my nerves and adrenaline still pumping through my system.

"What happened?" Tracey finally asked as she put the car in park.

Where did I even start? "Everything was going great and the chemistry was there. I swear I had never felt like I did in that car. No man or boy or anything had ever made me feel so good." I paused to swallow and get my wits about me.

Tracey leaned over and grabbed my hand in hers and then I smelled it. My wolf smelled it. I knew immediately it was guilt. She was feeling guilty over this happening again. I squeezed her hand in mine before I continued. "Then he pressed his teeth to my neck and something wasn't right. I felt like everything was wrong."

Tracey's brows pulled together as her eyes looked at my neck. My neck still hadn't healed and the blood was still wet there. "That isn't normal. You said you didn't feel a mate's bond? He shouldn't have tried to claim you like that. Something is definitely wrong." Her eyes flicked to the Manor in front of us and there was Rafe's mom. She held up a little towel and a first aid kit. "As soon as Rafe left to follow you," She stopped and I pondered on her words. Rafe had followed me from the party. "I came back here. There was no use in me following too. I don't like to watch other people and I figured Rafe was just going to check on you. He screamed down the Alpha link and I knew something wasn't right."

"Wait," I held my hand up to her. "You didn't leave before us?"

Tracey blinked slowly and shook her head. Her

curls bounced with the movement. "No, I was waiting on you. I wasn't even the one that noticed you were gone from the party. It was Rafe."

Carden had lied. Why wasn't I surprised? I blinked then blinked again as I tried to process all of this. The Manor was empty as we walked into it. Save for, Alice, Rafe's mom. She sat at the large dining table, watching and waiting. Her mouth was set in a grim line as she watched us approach. Alice nodded once and Tracey threw herself into one of the chairs at the table, I did the same. I startled hard as a pitcher of lemonade appeared in front of us. Two glasses were already half full. Tracey shrugged with a small smile on her face.

"Perks of being a witch, I guess."

Alice smirked. "You're more wolf than witch."

Tracey leaned back as she sipped from the glass. She didn't say anything back to Rafe's mom and I didn't know what to say either. So I just sat there and stared at the pitcher as the ice cubes melted. Exhaustion pulled at my brain but all I could do was stare.

Alice broke through my mindless stupor. "We should probably clean your neck."

I only blinked at her as she got up with a first aid kit and came to my side. I didn't say anything as she cleaned the blood from the side of my neck and then put a bandage over it. "The wolfsbane is probably preventing you from healing." Her eyes flashed to Tracey and my friend grimaced.

"Did I do something wrong?" I had to ask, I had to make sure. I knew I had already done something wrong by trusting *another* wolf bad boy. But who could blame me? Maybe these men were just a bad batch. I sighed as Alice thought over her words carefully.

"No, but Tracey knew better. We don't permit wolfsbane outside of the pack lands. This is how bad things happen. All you need is a little in your system and then small superficial wounds won't clot. Wolfsbane has many good uses but sometimes the younger wolves forget that it can also kill you. Thankfully, Granny is the one that mixes all of our alcohol so I trust that there is no lethal amounts in it, but still. It renders us vulnerable all the same."

Tracey pressed her lips together.

I jumped as the front door slammed open. Rafe leaned in the doorway and my heart stopped. He was a bloodied mess from his head to his toes. His clothes were shredded and offered him little modesty. His tattoos extended well past his arms and to his chest and what looked to go down his abdomen. How much pain had he endured for his art?

"He was a rat," Rafe spat. "The glamour fell away from him as soon as I bit into his skin and tasted the magic in his blood."

I swallowed before I inhaled hard. Rafe was injured and it wasn't healing.

Alice's spine straightened. "What of Carden? Where is he?"

Rafe's smile was ruthless and full of malice. "I dropped him off at Granny's." Like it was something innocent but the look of horror on Tracey's face told me everything I needed to know. Granny wasn't going to take it easy on my date.

"Glamour?" The question slipped past my lips. I was still reeling from Tracey magically poofing lemonade into the room. How much more could I take? How long would it take before nothing surprised me anymore?

Rafe swallowed and I watched as his sharp jaw tilted up. His eyes searched my face before they painstakingly ran down my neck and snagged on the bandage there. I could have sworn molten rage filled his gaze before he blinked and looked away. What was his game? "The tattoos, the piercings, and whatever else had you attracted to him wasn't real."

My mouth went dry. His jaw clenched as his eyes roved over me again. I looked away. I didn't care. I didn't want his attention, I didn't need him to avenge me. I didn't need anything from him, not now and not ever. "He had strong magic in his blood. This was a ploy."

"Where is the rest of the Bruiser Pack?" Rafe's mom asked. I just couldn't get past the part where everything in this night had been fabricated and not real.

Rafe ran his tongue over his teeth. "I spoke with Gamble already. They're leaving and they're leaving their traitor with us."

I had thought I had heard Rafe angry, I thought I had seen his many faces and masks. But I wasn't prepared for the icy tone in his voice.

Then I remembered. "You were watching us. Are you a voyeur or something?" I pushed my fingers into my hair. "Why can't you just stay away from me?"

A growl sounded from behind me and I jumped as Alice spoke in a booming, growly voice. "I know he isn't *your* Alpha but he saved your life. He didn't have to. That wolf was likely out for blood. You should be thanking Rafe."

I took a deep breath. I wasn't going to back down.

I wasn't going to be gaslighted. I had a right to be upset. Rafe had already taken so much from me. He wasn't going to take my voice too. I shoved my chair away from the table and stalked to him with my finger raised. "I don't care who you are. You have violated my trust countless times and now this. Let's not even get started on why I am even here. I am here because of you and I don't want to be." Tears burned my eyes as I jabbed him in the chest. I ignored the feel of his warm firm chest as I did so. "I didn't *ask* for any of this. Excuse me if I am trying to just live a normal life. I didn't ask for a Mate's Meet or whatever that is. I just happened to be in the wrong place at the wrong time. *Again.*"

CHAPTER 32

I didn't care about what anyone said as I marched out of the Manor and looked for my car. The moisture that had been burning my eyes was now spilling over. My shoulders shook as I realized that I didn't have my car. That I had ridden with Carden to the party and then with Tracey back to the Crimson's property. I couldn't call this pack lands. Not yet. They weren't my people. Even if Rafe had saved my tail. I couldn't admit to anything yet. My senses were starting to come back stronger now that the wolfsbane was leaving my system. I could almost feel my neck patching itself back together under the bandage. I swiped at the tears under my eyes and stalked to the line of the woods. I wasn't going to ask any more from this pack. I wasn't going to continue to inconvenience them. There was nothing left for me to do but go home.

Exhaustion continued its assault on me as I trudged through the darkness. I could practically smell the roasted tofu and knew that my senses would bring me home. I had to learn to trust this extra part of myself, even if it was foreign. I was thankful for a moment that I had worn Converse.

The hairs on the back of my neck stood up. I knew he was there before he said anything. "What do you want?" I whipped around.

Rafe left the shadows of the trees behind me and shoved his hands into his pockets. He had changed and was no longer in torn clothing. "These woods aren't safe. I wanted to make sure you got home."

"Why do you care?" I turned back around and continued in the direction of my home. It couldn't be that far.

"I did save your ass tonight, I would like to see that all of these cuts, bruising and pain are worth something. If you die after I went through all of that, what's the point?" He snickered but I could still smell the blood on him. It wasn't Carden's.

"You aren't healing," I kept walking. If he wanted to talk he would have to follow me.

"No, wolfsbane will do that to you and whatever other magic he had in his blood. I could hardly get out of my wolf form once I got him down."

"I didn't see you drinking tonight," I hadn't thought the Alpha would have put himself in such a compromising position.

"You didn't see a lot of things tonight." His voice was clipped and he was right but how was I supposed to know my date was glamoured?

"My senses healing has come back, why hasn't yours?" I knew the answer before he muttered it.

"I drank *a lot* more than you did."

I nodded my head, unsure of what to say now. But then he surprised me. "I'm sorry for watching. I didn't mean to. I don't trust the Bruiser Pack and I wanted to make sure you were safe."

"I didn't pledge to your pack." I shrugged. It didn't make any sense. I didn't want to think that I needed him to keep me safe, but after tonight, there was a part of me that was relieved he had shown up. What would have happened if he hadn't?

"No, you didn't, but I turned you and I feel responsible. I just wanted to make sure. My instincts are never wrong. If he hadn't put his teeth on you and you hadn't told him to stop, I would have left. I want you to know that." His voice was soft, almost a whisper. "I wouldn't have stayed." I looked at him then. His eyes were a soft honey and his head was mostly angled away from me. His jaw was clenching and unclenching.

"I don't understand you, Rafe."

"I just want to keep you safe." Then he was gone and I couldn't wrap my mind around the conversation we had. There hadn't been any anger or fear. I sighed as I walked around the fence that labeled my yard. I tried to rub under my eyes to make sure no makeup was smeared there but they would know.

I was walking up the driveway when the front door opened. My mom was the first to rush out. "Are you okay?"

They had seen the smudged mascara on the cameras. I nodded my head as her arms wrapped around me and I smelled home. My shoulders relaxed as I took a deep breath. She smelled like oats and honey. Everything that kept me calm and right. My dad was out the door next and my heart lurched at the sight. My stomach did a flip-flop when I noticed the shotgun grasped between his hands. I let out a wheezing laugh as I looked between my helicopter parents. I shook my head as my mom's arms squeezed me back into a tight embrace.

"Did he hurt you?" My dad's voice boomed as my

mom escorted us into the house. Her small hands rubbed up and down my arms. I wanted to bottle up the comfort and save it for later. Deep inside of me, I knew I was going to need it.

CHAPTER 33
RAFE CRIMSON

The bark on the tree dug into one of the cuts on my arms as I leaned into it. Jade's light was on in her bedroom and the curtains fluttered in the wind. I had been surprised when I watched her open the window but then her eyes had found mine in the darkness and I wondered if she had done it to locate me. Her wolf was growing stronger each day and eventually, she would be able to find me without much effort. I didn't hide that much but in the beginning, I hadn't wanted her to know I was watching.

I was always watching and I hated myself for it.

CHAPTER 34

Saturdays were my favorite. It meant I could sleep in, I didn't have to worry about much and my parents were extra cheery. They had another vacation on the horizon and were going to be extra chatty about it. I stretched my arms wide over my head and smiled sleepily. My parents hadn't left me alone all night, and even when they had *left me alone*, my mom peeked into my room several times throughout the night to make sure I was okay.

I had explained the tears the best I could. I got my hopes up for a boy that wasn't worth it. I had wasted my time on someone that just didn't care if he hurt me. Which wasn't a lie but also wasn't all of the truth. I didn't mention that I had cried over my humanity being taken from me or that I had to see the villain every single day or the fact that I was lying to them at every turn. I couldn't explain that I cried over the part of me that knew I needed to move out but I didn't know how I possibly could. I had to be honest with them but what would I say? They loved taking care of me and I knew they would never be ready for the day that I had to move into the real world but that day was quickly approaching.

My sleepy smile disappeared as I kicked the blankets from my legs and rose from the bed. I looked at the clock and the good mood I had woken up with disappeared. It was five A.M. In what lifetime did I enjoy waking up this early? I could practically feel my wolf purring. It seemed like she loved waking up early.

The hot spray of the shower was the only thing that brought me relief. I stayed under the water until the showerhead pelted me, with what felt like, ice. I shivered and stepped from the tub.

My phone rang from my bedside table and the sound of it shocked my, once again, sensitive senses. I clicked it onto speaker while I pulled my clothes on.

"How are you feeling?" Tracey's voice was soft as it blasted through my room.

"I have had better mornings," I muttered.

"Granny got some information out of Carden," I could hear the hesitation in her voice like she wasn't supposed to tell me any of this. Like she was considering what else she would tell me.

"Do I need to come by?" I didn't want to. That was the last thing I wanted to do on my Saturday but I would do it. I wanted answers. I needed them. Why would he pretend and then why would he hurt me like that? There had been zero signs leading up to it.

Tracey blew out a breath into the speaker and I winced at the sound. "Yeah, that would probably be best."

My parents were in the kitchen making a vegan hash when I came down the stairs. The smell of it turned my stomach. I had considered eating breakfast with them but not anymore. "Good morning, honey!"

I smiled at them tentatively. "Good morning," I had my bag slung over my shoulder already.

"Where are you headed this early?" My dad asked as he put his iPad down and then his reading glasses beside it.

It was time to rip off the bandaid. "I need to go to the city and apply for some internships."

My dad blinked and then my mom chuckled. "You have another year of college."

I shrugged. "My ambassador told me that I needed to apply."

"Is that the smartest idea? You have everything taken care of here." My father's salt and pepper brows pulled together in the center.

I sighed. I should have known better. They weren't going to let me do this easily. "Yes, but eventually I will have to take care of myself. I will need to get a job and my own place to live."

My mom put her hand over her chest like it pained her to hear these words. It probably did but there was nothing I could do about it. I had to grow up eventually. "That isn't true. We have loved taking care of you. We have more than enough money to do so too."

I pressed my fingers into my temples and rubbed the skin there. "I have loved every second of you taking care of me and I appreciate it more than you could ever know."

"But?" My dad encouraged and my mom shot him a death glare.

"But, I want to be able to take care of myself. I want to have friends and responsibilities. Maybe even a cat." Internally I was laughing to myself. I would probably never get a cat but I knew it would rub my mom the wrong way. She was allergic and had always wanted me to have a pet. *Little did she know.*

Mom looked away from me to her uneaten hash. "I hate that we never let you get one."

I leaned forward and put my hand on hers. "I can have one if I get my own place."

Dad nodded like it made sense like my argument had moved him but I wondered what he would counter with later. I had to be convincing on this. "You're not our little baby anymore, even though we want you to be. I want you to be self-sufficient in this world. I need you to be. We won't be here forever, you're right but I want to look into these places that accept you for interning. Only the best for my little girl."

Tracey was waiting for me at her Granny's. My chipper friend was exceptionally somber today. Whatever they had found out wasn't good. I turned to go into Granny's cottage and Tracey's hand on my arm stopped me. "You don't want to go in there."

I shrugged her touch off. I could smell the blood

in the air, I knew what I was going to find on the other side of the door. My fingers wrapped around the brass doorknob and the door swung open. On the back wall of the home was Carden. His hands were chained up and away from his body. His legs were spread and chained to the floor. The Carden I was looking at wasn't the Carden I had gone out with the night before. His face was a bruised and bloody mess. He was shirtless and a sheet covered the lower half of his body. I took a tentative step forward and the smells in the room assaulted me.

Blood, piss, vomit, and something else. Something that smelled much worse than the others. I covered my nose and my mouth with my hand as Granny came out of a room on the left side of the cottage. Her thick hair was pulled away from her face and she wore a plain dress. She looked like she had stepped out of the 1700s. She didn't look at me as she spread out items on the floor in front of the wolf.

"Why is he naked?" My voice came out in a squeak. The last thing I needed to be was concerned. My fingers itched to touch the sensitive skin on my neck. It had healed enough for the bandage to come off, but it was still fresh in my mind. I shivered.

Tracey leaned against the doorway. "He wouldn't

shift back last night, even after Rafe beat him. Even after Rafe wrapped his teeth around his neck."

Carden's eyes were closed and his head lolled forward but a low groan came from his lips. When his eyes blinked open they were completely black. I took a step back and considered running. Considered leaving this place and all the nightmares that came with it.

Tracey's hand on my shoulder stopped me. "Granny is going through his memories. It could take a little while. He admitted last night that he was drugged. A witch is involved and we have to find out who."

"Why though?" My fingers finally found the spot. The spot that he had tried to bite.

"If you're claimed, you can't be claimed again." The dark words came from Carden's mouth but they were anything but Carden's voice.

I gasped as Granny fell to the ground and started to seize. Tracey was by her side in seconds, all while Carden's black, soulless eyes watched me. I couldn't move or think as the beast watched me. Whoever was on the other side of those eyes used Carden's mouth to grin. "What do you want? Why would he try to claim me?"

The grin stretched wider and terror filled me. I

grasped my hands together to keep them from shaking as I faced down a monster. "To keep you from being claimed by your true mate, silly. We want a lot of things but aren't at liberty to share them right now."

Granny went still on the floor and the blackness leaked from Carden's eyes. I hadn't allowed myself to look at him, really look at him, until that moment. The piercing that had been in his brow was gone, no scar to even suggest that there had been one there. The tattoos that had snaked all over his body were nowhere to be seen either. The man hanging before me was someone else entirely. When he blinked his eyes open all I saw was green, I knew that the man I had been intrigued with was a fake.

The chains around his hands and ankles jingled as he fought consciousness. "Where am I?" Even his voice sounded different. Lighter.

Granny pulled herself from the rugged floor and wiped her hand across her brow. She clenched and unclenched her jaw while she tried to find the words.

"Carden?" My voice was soft, hesitant.

His eyes snapped to mine and fear filled them. "What happened? Where am I? Who are you?"

He didn't remember me. His questions were

those of truth. I could taste it in the air. He truly didn't know who I was. Granny straightened her back and stepped between us.

"Carden, I need you to tell me the last thing you remember." Her voice was hard and unyielding. She didn't act like a woman that had just been seizing moments before. Her voice was strong, even as Tracey lingered near her, prepared to catch her if things went wrong. Tracey's shoulders were tight, while her feet were spread in a fighting stance.

Carden blinked before he tested the chains again. "A woman told me to hold still while," he paled and a red flush filled his cheeks. "She, um, well." He stopped again. "We were hooking up and she told me to be still then another woman came in. I thought it was my lucky day and then there was blinding pain through my body. The other woman that had come in was standing over me, whispering words in another language and I remember thinking that I had stumbled into the wrong kink house. Is that how I got here?"

Tracey looked over her shoulder at me and took a deep breath. "We need to get Gamble on the phone. Go get Rafe."

I could see the regret in her eyes. She didn't want

to send me out to my enemy for help but I knew I didn't have a choice. We needed more answers than what this man could give us and Tracey wasn't going to leave her grandmother's side. I nodded once and ran as fast as I could to the Crimson Manor.

CHAPTER 35
JADE RIVERS

Rafe watched all of us carefully as he replayed what had happened on the phone and everything Gamble had told him. "Carden was a forced change." He wouldn't look at me. "A forced *claiming*." At that admission, there was a collective gasp around the room. "A dark witch was involved with the night he was it was forced on him and took over his mind. The man has been with the Bruiser Pack for almost a year."

Nausea swirled within my gut. The man didn't even know. He had no idea he was a wolf and all this time had gone and he had no idea what had happened. He couldn't remember anything. He had been forced to change and claimed in a mating bond and had zero say in the matter. He would never know his true mate now, if he even wanted that.

Granny had forced herself into the tiny dark corners of his mind, but it did nothing. She couldn't find the face of the wolf that had done all of this to him. The magic that had bound him seemed to be gone from his system but Granny wanted to make sure. She put a binding spell on his mind, whatever that meant, and released him from the chains. Someone had brought him clothes but he still hadn't left the witch's cottage. I didn't blame him, he was about to have his world rocked.

I shoved my fingers through my hair while Rafe continued on with the semantics. All while he paced at the head of the dining table. The room was packed full and barely contained all of the wolves that lived within the pack.

"Because of this," Rafe shoved his hands into his pockets. "We will no longer be letting any strangers onto pack lands. For those of you that work on pack lands with the public, you will be relocated to another job temporarily. Or we will change the borders on the land. I don't know what to do to make this easier for all of you but I know that I must protect you. Mate Meets will no longer happen until we can get this all investigated. All pack members that are out of town or visiting other territories will be called back and undergo a quarantine period. If they want to be trusted and allowed within the pack, Granny will be looking through their thoughts and looking for magical tethers."

I bit my lip from asking what all this meant. If she had done all of this before, would they had known Carden was possessed? I leaned back in my chair and Tracey's hand found mine under the table. I still hadn't pledged to be a part of this pack but I was being treated as if I had. I squeezed her hand in mine and looked to where our hands were joined. All while Rafe talked he didn't once mention what I had told them. That they were trying to prevent me from being claimed by my true mate. He hadn't said anything as the words had spilled from my lips. His face had gone pale and he stormed away. Tracey had been there to hug me fiercely and I knew without a shadow of a doubt that I needed her and her strength or I was never going to survive.

The walk to my car seemed to take forever. The forest was alive again and I couldn't stop myself from listening to every detail I had missed before. The loud sound of my boots crunching against the gravel or the birds chittering to each other in the trees. And even though I had been able to pick up on those sounds before I was turned. It was different now. It was louder and had more feeling, more depth. Even though Rafe was light on his feet, I could hear him approach behind me. I paused at my car door.

"I know I have no right to ask this of you, but I would like it if you could stay on pack lands until we can figure all of this out. It's directly related to you and something isn't sitting right with me. I can't protect you out there." He sighed and closed his eyes and for a moment- a brief one- I wanted to reach out and touch him. Comfort him. But I didn't. I kept my hands to myself and leaned against the side of my car.

"I have to go to school and I have internships I need to apply for." My voice sounded like I was on the fence. Like I was considering his words.

"What if they come after you again?" He clenched his jaw and I wasn't sure if it was because he was angry or irritated.

"Then I am the single line of defense between them and my family. My two defenseless, *human* parents. Or did you forget that I didn't choose this life?" It was a low blow but one that needed to be said. I had to remind the both of us of the elephant in the room. I wouldn't let him get away with it, even if I did feel bad about the pressure on his shoulders.

He ran his hands down his face and his shoulders slumped. "You're right, I'm not your Alpha but I worry about you."

The smile that spread across my face was anything but friendly. "You don't have that right, not after everything you have taken from me."

I got in my car and was closing my door when I heard the whisper or maybe it was my imagination but I couldn't shake it all the same. "What about all the things I have given you?"

The question that Rafe had asked continued to burn through my thoughts as I sat down with my parents that night for dinner and as I tossed and turned in my bed afterwards. What had he given me? I had heightened senses yes, but what else? I didn't know what that meant and I didn't know how to answer it for myself.

There was a knock on my door before my dad stepped into my bedroom. He was so fragile, so human. It scared me for him and also made me envious. I wished I could go back to the fragile naivety. I longed for the ignorance he had. Witches, werewolves, and vampires were real and they were haunting me. Even more so now that I knew I was being hunted.

"Are you okay?" He kept asking me that. He

knew, he could see it, that I wasn't the same girl I had been months ago. I wasn't the same girl they had left here but there was nothing I could do about it.

Imposter.

I sat up in bed and turned the bedside lamp on. It cast the room in a soft yellow glow. I plastered on my best fake smile. "Yeah, why do you ask?"

Dad blinked and then he sighed. "You hardly eat anymore and you look different."

I had to hold my hands together to keep from touching the fresh mark on my neck. I leaned back into my pillows, casually. "How do I look different?"

He narrowed his eyes like he wasn't sure if he was right about it but said it anyway. "Like you have bulked up almost but at the same time, lost weight."

I would have to explain something to him. He was right. I had chosen to ignore the changes in my body but they were there especially as I lounged in my bed in my pajamas. My legs were more defined and so were my arms. There was a healthier glow to my skin, even though I had been sick when they came home. Now I felt better than I had ever felt before. I was stronger mentally and physically. I was excelling in my classes and retaining knowledge like I never had before. I had to spin this lie perfectly. If I didn't, he would know. "I have been working out with Tracey after class."

It would explain my extra absences and he wouldn't worry about me partying like they had before. But he also checked his account like a hawk and I had no money of my own. Another thing looming over my head. If I had a gym membership, he would have called me out about the charges. I tried to charge as little to their account as I could and if I needed to hide anything, I always ordered from Amazon or got cash from the ATM in small increments. Not that I had hidden much. But I didn't exactly want my dad to know about my lingerie or where I bought it from.

"I was wondering, you look good." Then he considered what he said. "I mean you have always looked good, but you seem healthier."

"We have been getting dinner after our workouts so I'm not really hungry after." I would leave it understood that Tracey was the one buying dinner but then his next question had me embarrassed.

"Are you two..." He fought with the words. "Seeing each other?"

I snorted. I should have seen that question coming. "I did go out with a guy last night."

Had it just been last night that everything had

happened? It felt like an eternity had passed. He waved his hand. "I had a best friend in high school that was gay and he pretended to go out on dates with women so his parents wouldn't know. I just want you to know that you never have to hide anything like that from us, that we will always accept you, no matter who you love."

Would you still accept me if you knew *what* I was?

Tears stung my eyes at his accepting tone. "You don't have to worry about that. Tracey has just been there for me through everything and I enjoy her company. She keeps the wild tamed."

He smirked. "You mean the partying?"

"Potato, patato," I countered.

"We are going to Morocco next, you should come with us." His words held a magical lilt to them. He was more excited about this trip than any of the others. I didn't blame him. Morocco was on my list and he knew it, that's why he was inviting me now. But with my wolf and everything happening, I didn't think it was a good idea.

"Maybe next time, Dad," I tried to conceal my sadness but I knew he could feel it.

He padded into the room and leaned down to kiss my forehead. "We leave next week, I just wanted to make sure that you knew you were always welcome to come with us."

I smiled as he retreated from my bedroom. "I have school and a future to think about. Maybe someday you can show me all the wonders of the world."

Maybe someday when my wolf was under control and I didn't feel like such an imposter. Maybe someday if they knew what and who I was, and they accepted me. Until then I would be here, trying to figure out one day at a time.

"Get some rest, kiddo." He closed the door and I flicked the lamp off.

Even in the darkness, I couldn't rest so I laid in the dark until the sun came up and shined through my window. I rose from the bed like I hadn't been awake all night and got in the shower.

My phone rang on my nightstand and I smiled. I wasn't even a tad tired as I wrapped my long hair into a towel and piled it on my head.

Crisscross applesauce is how I found myself later that afternoon, with a bunch of preschoolers. They were learning about their wolves today and Tracey figured it would be the best opportunity for me to learn. I sat in between two little girls that couldn't stop giggling with each other. I was supposed to be the buffer, but I didn't think it was working very well. They would both look at each other then look at me and burst into a fit of hysterics. They were cute little things with pigtails and bows in their hair but they were certainly mischievous too. I ignored them the best I could to paid attention to Tracey's mother, Vivian. Her pale hair was pulled back into a loose knot on the back of her neck and her face was bare from any makeup.

"As a werewolf we are stronger, faster, and healthier than our human neighbors. We heal at a faster rate and their sicknesses do not affect us either. How many of you have been feeling more hungry as of late?"

A few children raised their hands around me. There were probably ten of them, which was odd to me because the pack hadn't seemed that big when I had been here before but then I remembered what was said about there being jobs on the pack lands. I probably hadn't seen even half of the pack because of that.

Vivian continued on with the lesson. "Your wolf is a part of you now and because of that, you will consume more food than an average human does.

You will need more water too. Your wolf will require much from you but in return, your wolf will provide. Your senses will be heightened, your body will be stronger, and with your wolf you are *immortal*."

Blood rushed into my ears at the sound of that. *What?* My eyes searched Vivian's but she just kept a small smile on her lips as she watched the little children around me. This was how they dropped the ball on me? Around a bunch of children? I breathed heavily through my nose as I tried to ground myself. I was going to throttle Tracey, then I was gonna go after Rafe *again*. What had he given me? A whole lot of shit that I wasn't prepared for is what he gave me.

Vivian's question quieted my thoughts. "Who knows what immortal means?"

The little girl to my left raised her hand. Vivian nodded in our direction and the little voice wrapped around me in a sweet embrace. "It means that we will live forever to protect our human neighbors. We are their guardians."

Then the rubber band in the center of my chest snapped again. Guardians?

Vivian's grin confirmed it. "Yes. There are other races out there that would harm the humans. The humans that are so close to what we are. If we don't protect them, no one will."

It had been a week since I had started the preschooler's class. I had learned far more than I thought I would. I was still excelling at my college courses and thankfully, with a forged doctor's note from Tracey, I was able to do all of my school work at home. But by home, I mean mainly at the Crimson pack lands. My parents worked from home and if I didn't at least act like I was going to school, there would be some major questions. Questions I didn't have answers to. Not yet at least.

My heightened senses were seeming to level out and the smell of my mother's vegan cooking didn't make me want to run away anymore. But I still ate dinner with Tracey and the pack. Even though Rafe had given the order for all of us to stay on pack lands or in my case, home, he had disappeared on *official*

Alpha business. Which left me to enjoy my time in peace and my pup classes without his haughty smirk peeking through the window every day. I could do without him lurking in the shadows.

I brushed my hair away from my face and felt it. The pain stabbed right through my middle and brought me to my knees. I fought to keep my eyes open against the rolling of pain throughout my body. I had a few more days till the full moon. We had expected my wolf wouldn't come till then and my parents would be out of town. They hadn't left yet...

The first crack of my bones seemed to echo around the room. My breathing became labored as I dragged myself across the floor to my phone and my laptop. I turned the music up as loud as I could without causing panic and dialed the first number I could as another crack sounded. The phone rang once before it fell from my hands and I threw up into the little trashcan beside my bed. When Tracey finally picked up I couldn't even speak. My body continued to contort and pop on the floor. I hoped and prayed that the music covered the sounds of my body transforming.

Why couldn't my wolf wait? Just a few more days... We had a few more. Agony ripped through me and I let out a pain-filled groan into the phone. Sweat dripped down my brow as I struggled to tell Tracey what was wrong. "My wolf is coming early."

Tracey swore on the other end. "How much longer do you have?"

Tears were streaming down my face now. Was it supposed to be this bad? "Maybe a few minutes."

There was a knock on my door and my entire body seemed to pause at the sound. Could my wolf wait it out for a few more minutes? "Your music is kind of loud. Do you need anything?"

I managed to drag myself across the carpeted floor to the bathroom just as my mom opened my bedroom door. "Jade?" She knocked on the bathroom door and I managed to swallow down some of my panic.

I struggled to get to the bathtub as another crack went through me and my music was turned down. *No, no, no, no.* "Yes, I'm fine, just some nerves about the finals coming up."

Somehow my voice didn't shake but the rest of my body was. "Okay, well please let me know if I can bring you anything."

"Uh-huh," A shiver went down my body and nausea held me tightly in its grasp.

A few seconds later there was a knock on the

door again. My body shook too hard for me to even answer. I threw up in the toilet as the door opened. Another pop sounded and I cried out. This was it, the moment my mother would find it all out. Except it wasn't my mom in the doorway, it was Rafe. His face was blank but his arms hung at his sides.

"I called Tracey," I choked out.

"Tracey went to the city for me to pick someone up from the airport. She didn't think you would appreciate her parents coming here. We are a little short-staffed at the moment."

I scowled at him as I threw up again. This time he detached himself from the wall and knelt by my side. A long second passed before he brushed my hair from my face and pulled it back to keep from falling in the toilet. As he ran his hand down my back in slow circles my wolf seemed to calm. The pops and cracks of my bones weren't as loud and the nausea was gone.

"What do I do?" I whispered.

His hands wrapped around the tops of my arms while he helped pull me from the bathtub. My legs shook too hard for me to climb out on my own. He helped lift me out without any problems, like I weighed nothing. His eyes were bright yellow when I looked up at them. Something inside of me shrunk away in fear and I knew it was because of what happened at the party when he turned me... and when he had saved me just a week ago.

"You let your wolf control the change. The more anxiety or fear you have, the worst it will be," he said as I stumbled but instead of hitting the ground, he swooped me up into his arms. My head lolled back as another pop ripped through me. I didn't even have the strength to look down at myself to see what I was becoming.

"What about my parents?" I growled through gritted teeth.

Rafe shushed me. "Don't worry about them. I can hear them if they head this way and can be out the window in seconds. I will keep you and them safe through this."

Pain ripped through me and a howl tore from my lips. Rafe looked nervously at my bedroom door as he laid me on the bed. "I'll be honest, this is the first time I've ever platonically laid a girl down."

He chuckled and I took a swipe at him. He managed to evade my punch then he settled down in the desk chair beside my open window. I was pretty sure I kept it closed and locked. I didn't even want to know how he had managed to get around that. Slowly, ever so slowly my body started to break, truly break. A whimper escaped my lips and my back bowed as everything happened all at once. The pain wasn't as bad as it had been before but it was steadily getting worse. Until the last pop and crack sounded and everything was different.

In one blink everything was black and white. My nose twitched on my much longer snout and something thumped behind me on the bed. I turned my head and there it was... a massive fluffy tail on the bed behind me. I blinked at it all slowly. Everything made sense but didn't. I could hear my parents talking downstairs but it was like there was a disconnect that my wolf couldn't put together. She pressed our ears to our head and let out a little whine. Why couldn't we understand what my parents were saying?

"Being a wolf will take some time to get used to." Rafe stood up from the chair in the corner and approached us. He held his hands up in surrender but my wolf didn't seem threatened by him.

My Alpha. She whispered in my mind. It was almost a purr of approval.

I scoffed. *Definitely not.*

There was a crash downstairs and my wolf jumped from the bed. The scent in the air was wrong. Something was wrong. Rafe held his hands up again and shook his head. "I will go check every-thing out."

I shook my massive head. He would get caught. He couldn't get caught here.

The corners of his lips pulled up into an almost smile. "I will be careful."

Before I knew what was happening, Rafe was out the window, there was a snarl from somewhere in the house and my parents were shouting. Their voices rose up through the floor in panic. My breathing became rapid as I paced around the room. How would I change back? Could I change back? What if they came up here while I was this massive animal? I got down on all fours and scooted my wolfish form under the bed then turned around to watch the door. My white paws jutted out in front of me and I stared at them in awe. This was a part of me. I could hardly believe it.

CHAPTER 38
JADE RIVERS

The panicked voices rose louder and then there were sirens in the distance. The wrong scent in the air only grew worse. Then Rafe was swinging his body back through my window in a quick arch and was on the floor in front of me.

"*Shift*," he commanded. I let out a whine.

I shook my head once.

"I know I am not your Alpha, Jade but you have to shift right now or there are going to be lots of questions about this massive animal that has taken your place." He stood up, peered over the side of the bed, and then chuckled. "You're literally tenting the center of your mattress right now. Jade, it will be painful but there was a break-in and your parents need you right now."

The words he spoke did it for me. I instantly felt

my wolf shrink back and even though there was pain, it wasn't nearly as much as before. A shiver raced down my spine as my limbs became shorter and smaller. The bed above me groaned as my wolfish body disappeared. I laid my head on my arms and took a deep breath. Rafe held out a scrap of silk material and I stared at it in bewilderment before I realized the shower was on. I could barely hear it over the blood roaring in my ears. I took the scrap of fabric, realizing it was my robe and I was lying underneath the bed naked.

I had forgotten that part. My cheeks flamed as he held his hand out to me but kept his eyes diverted. I hesitantly put my hand in his much larger one. In one jerk he yanked me out from under my bed, then shoved me into the bathroom. I leaned my forehead against the door as the sirens got closer to the house. Then his words came back to me and I jerked the door back open.

Rafe had disappeared again and my window was closed. I wrapped the pink robe around myself and rushed out of my bedroom as quickly as I could. I took the stairs two at a time as my heart pounded out of my chest. There was a knock at the door before I could make it to my parents. My mom was holding a bag of frozen vegetables to her face and my father was opening the door. I pulled the robe around myself more securely. My knees buckled with every step. My mom erupted into tears when she saw me. The bag of vegetables dropped from her hands and there was a black bruise forming around her right eye.

I frowned and rushed to her side. My hands hovered right over her face like there was something I could do about it. "What happened? I heard a crash just as I was about to get in the shower."

She laughed and shrugged her shoulders like she wasn't fragile. "An accident I think. Someone threw a ball through the kitchen window and it hit me while I was doing the dishes." The smell of wrongness was still heavy in the air. I inhaled deeply to try to catch the scent again, to try to distinguish what I was smelling. But it was no use.

"Someone came into our yard and threw a baseball through the window?" I blinked slowly as I looked toward dad at the front door. He was leading the policeman through the house and into the kitchen.

"Yes, officer, someone was in the yard when they threw the ball. It wasn't a fly ball that went over the fence. We don't have neighbors that even have younger children." My father's voice was filled with fury.

The policeman nodded his balding head as he surveyed the damage. "What about the cameras posted outside your home?"

My dad scratched his head, confused. "I looked at them but there was no one on them. I don't understand unless there was a blink where it didn't pick anything up."

The cop nodded his head before he picked the ball up with gloved hands. He put it into a baggy and then started his report on the clipboard that had been tucked under his arm. My mom pressed her hand to the small of my back and led me away from the broken glass in the kitchen. It was then that I realized I still wasn't dressed. I brushed my mother's light hair away from her face and took a deep breath.

"That looks nasty, please be careful." *You're too fragile.* My mom shrugged again and I felt a desperation rising within me. "Are you two still going to leave tomorrow?"

The front door closed and my father approached us in the spacious living room. "Yes, the police officer is checking around back but he doesn't believe there was ill intent. We can't change our flight but I'll be having someone come out tomorrow to check the cameras first thing in the morning."

I nodded my head and my mom kissed my hairline. "Go take that shower," She wrinkled her nose. "You smell like sweat and," She paused as she took another sniff at me. "Wet dog."

I raised my eyebrows and laughed. "That's gross, you're right, I should get to the shower."

My legs were slower going up the stairs as the adrenaline faded from my system. My muscles protested on the last step and I felt myself tilt sideways with exhaustion but before I could topple down the stairs Rafe was there wrapping his fingers around mine. He pulled me forward and into my room faster than I could blink. My door clicked closed behind us and my legs gave out. Every single muscle in my body ached. It felt like it was bone-deep. Rafe had me up in his arms before I could hit the ground.

"A forced shift isn't easy on the body and then you rushed down the stairs like that."

I didn't care about what he was explaining. I would go over that later. "Did you see what happened?" My voice sounded tired and I didn't know how I was going to be able to shower feeling like this.

Rafe's eyes flashed yellow. "I don't know what happened out there, but I will be getting that ball from the police station in the morning."

I rolled my eyes as he once again brought me to the bathroom and then set me down in the tub. He turned the water on and checked the temperature on the back of his hand before he walked out. All I could do was sit there and stare as the water poured in around me and my robed body. *Stupefied*. That's what he had done to me. Gone was the behemoth of a man that I was used to. Was I getting to experience the real Rafe? I leaned my head back in the tub and didn't worry about the robe floating around in the water. I could hardly move my legs or arms, the last thing I was worried about was the wet garment. I would figure it out when the time came for me to get out of the water. I leaned forward, with all of my strength, to turn the water off then practically fell backwards in exhaustion.

CHAPTER 39
RAFE CRIMSON

The rogue wolves were closing in. Whatever they had planned, they would start to take it out on the most fragile part of the pack. The one woman that had no idea she was putting herself in danger. She smelled like the Crimson Pack so they had gone after her first. I leaned against her window as the water shut off and went over my options.

I would have to stay close in order to protect her house through the night but I couldn't be in the woods. My wolf was powerful but not that much. I could only take on so much alone. I knew how to pick and choose my battles but I also knew that after a forced shift, Jade wouldn't be able to do much for herself. There was a loud splash in the bathroom before I heard Jade curse. I had been so lost in thought I hadn't heard her try to get out of the tub.

I didn't bother with knocking as I barged into the bathroom. Jade was laying face first on the tiled floor and her hair was a wet mess stuck to her face. The pink robe I had given her was clinging to her body in a way I couldn't even acknowledge at the moment. I forced my eyes away from her form and pulled a towel from the cabinet.

Before I could change my mind I wrapped the towel around her shoulders and pulled her from the floor. My lips tipped up in amusement. "How many times am I going to save your sorry ass?"

Jade squeezed her eyes shut and shook her wet hair against me. "You have a lot to make up for."

"Don't forget, I also gave you a lot too." Her eyes flashed yellow and it took all the self-control I had to gently place her back on her bed then rifle through her drawers for her pajamas.

She let out a squeak and I felt awful. She didn't deserve a forced shift and her wolf was probably freaking out right now. I grabbed the first things I saw and tossed them her way.

CHAPTER 40
JADE RIVERS

Rafe Crimson continued to surprise me again and again. He kept his back turned away from me while I very slowly dragged my pajamas up my damp body and then waited until I told him I was decent. The panty thief I had known wasn't present right now and it confused my foggy brain. When I was finished I didn't have the strength or the will power to even move. My eyes started to slide shut and my body ached all over. I had zero fight left in me when the bed dipped beneath Rafe's weight and he pulled the blankets over my body. I peeked up at him from beneath my lashes and there was a frown on his face. I wanted so desperately to tell him that he didn't have to be here but the fight was gone. I had no will to even care if he didn't want to be here and was doing this for Tracey's sake.

A sigh escaped me as Rafe leaned back on the pillow beside mine. My shoulders relaxed and then as my consciousness was leaving me, I could have sworn he twirled a piece of my hair around his finger.

The night before slammed into me as I jerked awake to an empty bed. I had actually shifted, which was a great surprise, but Rafe had stayed the night and I had no idea when he had left. Then there was the part about the run-in with my parents and I still wasn't sure if it was something I needed to be concerned about or not.

I dressed quickly and rushed down the stairs to find a group of strangers in my kitchen. Once again, the smell was off. It was wrong but I couldn't place why. I pulled the fridge open and wrapped my fingers around a bottle of water. I didn't bother with opening it as I listened to the conversation surrounding the window that had been broken the previous night.

The man beside the sink promised my father it would only take a few minutes to replace but his words stunk. They pulled at a memory from the preschooler's class. *We could taste lies.* But why was this man lying to my father?

I leaned against the fridge and watched the men milling in and out of the house as the main man assured my father that the job would be paid for by insurance and they had already gotten in touch with them. My father didn't look too relieved. His shoulders were straight and rigid. He wasn't going to leave until they were done with the job. The man at the sink looked at me and for a brief moment, his eyes flashed yellow and I *knew*. He was a wolf and that was the smell from the night before. I kept my face neutral as I leaned forward and kissed my father's cheek.

"I'm gonna go for a run," I rubbed my hand down his back and then walked away from the group of wolves that didn't belong in my house. Why they were there, I didn't know. But I needed to get to Rafe as soon as possible. I was thankful I had dressed in leggings and a loose shirt. I made a beeline for the woods and then let my body do the rest. I made it halfway through the woods when another body slammed into mine.

"Where you going little wolf? Run to visit grandma's house?" A man's voice sneered into my ear. He smelled like Tabasco and wolfsbane. I put my hands on my knees and panted hard.

"Actually I am, Granny has been missing me lately." A smile stretched across my face as the man circled me. He was a decent enough looking guy. He had a heavy build with a thick mop of brown hair on his head. His eyes flashed yellow. I didn't recognize this man from inside the kitchen but that didn't mean they weren't working together. My wolf wanted to come to the surface so badly to do the fighting for me but my body was too weak. Fur rippled along my arms but that was all she could do. The forced shift, I imagined, had drained me more than a regular shift would have but being a wolf with law enforcement in the house wouldn't have been a good thing.

"Where's your mate at? Did he run off to go play somewhere else?" I couldn't tell if the man was taunting me or not. His voice was cold and I knew he was going to attack at any moment. I couldn't let him catch me off guard.

I rolled my eyes as we circled each other. "What do you want?"

"There are many things that I *want*, but unfortunately you can't give me those things but maybe you can give me something else."

Nausea rolled through my stomach and the soreness in my body made it hard to stand but I had to get to the Pack. There was a group of werewolves in my kitchen and I had left my dad alone. I backed into a tree and almost threw up. I had left them alone with werewolves. What had I been thinking? My breath was coming out in short pants and I knew I had to get back home. That was more important than this stupid mission I had gone out on. But before I could think about slipping away to get back to my parents, a blur flashed before my eyes and the man in front of me was thrown through the air.

His body sailed a few feet before he was impaled on a tree branch above me. The blur stopped and there was another stranger before me. His auburn hair shone in the light that broke through the thick canopy of trees above us. He whipped his head my way and grinned. His eyes were yellow and his shirt was gone. On his right pectoral muscle, there was the stamp of the Crimson Pack crest. The face of a wolf on a shield with two spears crossed behind it. He held out his hand then chuckled before he pulled it back. In the center of his palm was a thick, red heart. My eyes immediately went up to the man impaled on the tree and I shuddered. The branches that he was hanging on were protruding from his shoulders. Then there was a gaping hole in the center of his chest.

The man that had saved the day made my blood go cold as he took a bite out of the heart in his hand. Blood poured down the sides of his lips as he spit the organ out of his mouth then threw it on the forest floor. I stumbled around the base of the tree as I took off in another run. I didn't know where I was going or what direction I was headed. All I knew was that I had to run. I couldn't get away fast enough and then I was being held in someone's arms that smelled like sunshine and flowers and a sob escaped my throat.

A hand ran down my hair as sobs wracked through my body. "Hey, it's okay, what happened?"

All I could do was shake my head as Tracey held me. Another scent overtook me and my body went taut. *Rafe.* I swiped my fingers under my eyes and tried to slow my breathing but the panic was still inside of me. Everything came tumbling from my lips and I *had* to get back to my parents.

I stumbled away from my friend and went to run back into the woods when she grabbed me on either side of my face to stop me. "Jade, it's okay, you're safe. Rafe has a few of our guards going to your parent's house. Their flight will be leaving soon, you'll need to say goodbye to them."

I nodded my head and took a deep breath. Yes, I couldn't let them know that I was breaking down. I needed ice. I pressed my palms into my eyes and after a few seconds Rafe had some ice cubes and a bottle of water. I wanted to ask him about the night before and how late he had stayed but I couldn't bring myself to do it.

Coward, my wolf whispered in my mind. I ignored her.

I took a sip out of the bottle of water and then the man from the woods sauntered out. There was still dried blood on his mouth and his hands were caked in it too. I swallowed hard and took a few steps back. I connected with Rafe's chest. His hands found my shoulders and steadied me. When had he become a comforting beacon?

When you realized there were worse monsters than him out there. My wolf was on a roll.

CHAPTER 41

JADE RIVERS

"So who was going to tell me that there was a newly changed wolf in the woods?" The bloodied man tilted his head as he looked at me. As he watched me with yellow eyes, another man I didn't recognize handed him a shirt and my lips pulled down.

Rafe chuckled. "I was going to tell you but you sensed the threat faster than I could."

The monster's nostrils flared and for a moment I felt a pull to him. "Who is she?" He tilted his chin up and I was able to get a better look at him. He had thick eyebrows over deep-set golden eyes, his jaw was sharp but covered in a red stubble. His auburn hair was combed away from his face and fell in waves against his thick neck.

I jutted my chin at him. "She is right *here*."

He smiled and my blood went cold as he inched

toward me. I licked my bottom lip and felt Rafe at my back again. This time I didn't back down. I wasn't afraid of this *man*. I cracked my neck and took a step toward him. He balked at me before he looked over my shoulder at his Alpha. "She's sigma."

My eyebrows wrinkled. "She is Jade and *she* doesn't like to be spoken about like she's not here." My tone dripped condescension.

Rafe let out a snort. Tracey raised her eyebrows as she looked around at everything but us. He took a step forward and grinned at me. I was surprised to find that his teeth were clean despite all the blood covering the rest of him. "I think you owe *me* a thank you."

It was my turn to snort. I shoved around him and headed back to the woods. My parents would be expecting me back at any moment and I had to be sure they were safe. Sitting here going head to head with another egotistical male was not what I needed to do. Tracey was quick on my heels. Thankfully she was in workout clothes and I wouldn't have to deal with questioning from my parents. They would probably be relieved to see Tracey. There was strength in numbers.

"Who is that guy?" I asked when we were far enough away from the pack lands.

Tracey scrubbed her hands down her face. "His name is Knox and he's a complete sweetheart."

I sputtered. "Could have fooled me."

I could smell the blood in the woods and made sure to avoid it the best I could. Tracey wrinkled her nose. "He's been training with the Pack Law the last year. Him and the rest of the Pack Guardians."

More terminology I didn't understand. "Pack Guardians?"

Tracey bit her lip. "I don't know if we should be discussing this."

I rolled my eyes as we broke through the other side of the woods. We stared at the back of my fence. We had to get this conversation rolling or it would be cut short as soon as my parents saw us. "Out with it."

"Rafe is next in line for Pack Law."

Chills erupted down my arms. "What?"

His father was seated on the Pack Law. They are the most powerful werewolves to ever exist."

I took a deep breath. This didn't affect me but then it did if I went to another pack and swore to another Alpha. He would always be there. I would always have to deal with him. But after my shift yesterday, would it be so bad? There had to an explanation, right?

"How was your shift last night?" Tracey changed the subject and I was grateful for it.

"Besides the person that broke the window, the wolves repairing my parent's home, and Rafe being the one to comfort me?" I shrugged. "Just dandy."

Tracey giggled and shook her head. "Why am I not surprised that it was eventful? I always miss the action. So how did he do? I really didn't want to send him but my hands were tied. I had to get Knox, Archer, Duncan, Gabriel, and Mav from the airport."

"Those are the Guardians?" I lowered my voice as we walked to the front of the house. All the cameras would be on nonstop now.

Tracey nodded. "Some of them, they are to protect our Alpha and the pack. I'm glad that they got back in time to deal with all of this. You think our senses are heightened? They can see farther, hear better, and track like no other."

My dad opened the door with a grin. "The weirdest thing happened today." He spotted Tracey and his smile grew. "Oh, hello!"

Tracey gave a little wave. "Hi, Mr. Rivers." She looked at me. "I'll be waiting in your room."

I gave her a nod.

"Those boys that were here before you left, there was something off about them." He shook his head as he closed to door behind me. "They left to go get the window out of their truck and completely disappeared."

My shoulders fell. That meant they wouldn't be leaving any time soon. But it was also a good thing because that meant that Rafe had managed to protect my parents. But when we walked into the kitchen I noticed that the window was as good as new. I frowned.

"That's where it gets weird. A few men knocked on the door a couple of minutes later and said they had been sent by Rafe Crimson, the Mayor's son. He said one of the kids on his property got lost last night and was spooked by something. They replaced the window within a few minutes and free of charge!" My dad did like free, but what kind of game was Rafe playing at here? Had it been one of his wolves that had done this? After seeing the rogue wolves in the kitchen and then the one in the woods, I knew that wasn't the case. Rafe and I would be talking soon. So I plastered on a fake smile and excitement. "Wow, that's awesome!"

"When we get back from Morocco, I want to go over to his property and thank him or maybe we can invite him and his family over for dinner." My heart ached to tell him. I pressed my lips together and continued to smile though.

"I think that would be great!"

Dad waggled his eyebrows at me. "I know you're nursing a broken heart but, I hear this Rafe fellow is quite the looker."

I swore the blood drained from my face. I rubbed my eyes to keep myself from bursting. The laughter was on the tip of my tongue. "Ya know, Dad, I'm just going to focus on myself for now. No boys."

Dad raised his eyebrows. "Girls then?"

The laughter spilled from my lips then. "No girls either."

He kissed the top of my head and passed me to the stairs. I could hear Mom above my head getting her final touches together. They would be on a long flight and my mom had her rituals for such things. She would need her special neck pillow, tons of snacks, and her blankets. There were probably other things she needed too but I had never stayed in the room long enough to watch her spaz out over it all. She made me anxious. She couldn't forget a single thing. I was glad Dad was going up there to make sure she wasn't forgetting anything.

Tracey was leaning against the wall when I

finally made it to my bedroom. She lifted an eyebrow at me. "So he was on the bed last night?"

My cheeks flamed. "It wasn't like that."

Tracey grinned. "Oh, I know. I can smell *that* too."

I rolled my eyes.

"What was he doing on the bed?" She shoved away from the wall and shook her shoulders like this was a good thing. This was *not* a good thing.

I sighed. "It was a rough shift. I don't know what happened. He wasn't the Rafe I was used to. I don't know." I looked at the ceiling while I scrubbed my hands down my face. "He was taking care of me."

Her light brows rose up on her forehead. "Rafe took care of you?"

I shrugged. "I don't know, I think. I fell asleep and he was still there. But he wasn't here when I woke up."

"You fell asleep while he was in your bed?" Her head jutted forward in disbelief while her eyebrows pulled together.

I hid behind my hands. "He forced a shift on me."

She blinked. "*Oh.*" She puffed her cheeks out. "Well, that explains why you fell asleep."

"But it wasn't even like that, even if I hadn't been exhausted." My shoulders slumped.

Tracey nodded as she sat on the edge of my bed. "Rafe is a good guy, even if he is broody and an ass."

I rolled my eyes. "You heard my dad talking about him and what he did for us."

Tracey gave me a sheepish grin. "Yes, but I also saw Rafe when he got back this morning. He looked like he was making the walk of shame."

"Did he look angry?" I bit my lip.

"He looked confused but then Knox tackled him to the ground and nothing else mattered."

"This Knox character..." I trailed off. He had probably saved my life, even if it was a terrifying way he had done it.

Tracey leaned back and kicked her shoes off. "He's a bit intense but as a Guardian of the Pack, he is more in tune with his wolf than anyone else."

"What did he mean when he said I'm a sigma?"

Tracey pressed her lips together. "I don't know if I'm the one that should tell you this."

I groaned. "You're my best friend, why wouldn't you be the right one to tell me?"

Tracey licked her lips. "Because I won't know for sure until you shift again. Your first shift was a bit hazy. I was trying to keep you from killing me." She sat up quickly and her eyes got big. "Oh my gosh, did you try to kill Rafe last night? Please tell me you did."

I shook my head and she fell back to the bed. Her hair created an arc around her shoulders as she connected with the mattress again. "No, my wolf was super content. It was an overall strange experience."

"Well, in any case, I won't be able to know until you shift again, which should be in a few days if your body feels ready again."

I rolled my shoulders. Most of the soreness had left my body and I sighed. I knew as soon as I took a hot shower or bath, the rest would fade away. "I think I should be ready to shift again on the full moon."

Tracey grinned. "You won't just be shifting, you'll be running with the rest of the pack. Are you sure you're ready for that?"

I pressed my lips together. "As long as Knox stays away from me, I should be okay."

Tracey laughed and shook her head against my pillow. "Well, Knox is exceptionally unpredictable. I can't speak for him, but I have a feeling he will be waiting for the prisoner to shift so he can get into his mind. The wolf mind is easier to get into than the human. Knox or Mav should be able to break the barrier on his thoughts. We have to know the witch that did this to him and possibly the wolf."

I had completely forgotten about Carden. "He doesn't have to shift?"

Tracey's eyes left my ceiling fan. "The Guardians do their training in their wolf form for over the course of a year. Think of it as SEAL training but more brutal. The ones that can't shift back at the end of it are executed."

My mouth dropped open. "Why?"

"Because their minds are broken and that's why their human half can't come back. Only the most powerful survive."

CHAPTER 42
JADE RIVERS

My parents had been gone two days and I was getting back into the swing of things even though Tracey kept bothering me to move onto the pack lands. Which was something I couldn't do. I needed to be self-sufficient. Moving in with the pack that wasn't even mine didn't scream independence. It screamed desperation. I needed a paying job. I needed responsibility for myself. I couldn't do that if I was still relying on others. I had all of my resumes typed up and printed out. *I could do this.* There was part of me that was a wolf but I wasn't going to harp on that. I could survive in this town and my life without constantly having to worry. I would live my life to the best of my capabilities. The rest be damned.

The doorbell rang and I threw my backpack over my shoulder. I frowned as I rushed down the stairs and peeked through the sheer curtains. I wasn't expecting anyone unless it was Tracey. But the massive figure on the other side of the door wasn't Tracey. I swung the door open, grabbed the man's hand, and yanked him into the house.

I didn't know who he was but I knew he was one of Rafe's Guardians. I let out a deep breath before I lit into him. "What are you doing here?"

His deep olive complexion stained pink for a moment before he shrugged his shoulders. "Hi, it's nice to meet you, too. My name is Mav."

I crossed my arms over my chest. "Hi, Mav, what are you doing here?"

Thankfully my parents had said service was spotty in Morocco and talking to them would be brief. I doubted they would be able to check the cameras if they could hardly get a call through.

He mocked my pose and crossed his arms over his chest. He was a big dude with tree trunk sized arms, thick neck, and a strong jaw. He didn't look like any wolves I was used to. He looked like he belonged on a beach doing the Haka somewhere tropical. His eyes were a pastel yellow as he looked me over. His hair was curly and bleached at the ends. He smiled and it was enough to ease *some* of the tension pumping through me.

"Tracey informed me that you would be going into the city today, I am here to escort you." I blinked slowly. That hussy ratted me out.

"This is some kind of joke, right?" I readjusted the purse on my shoulder. The last thing I needed was a babysitter, especially one that would be seeing where I was applying to work.

All he did was grin. "I can assure you that this isn't a joke."

"What if I say no?" I pinched my lips together as I tried to think of a clever way to get out of this.

Mav leaned back against the wall and crossed one ankle over the other. "I would suggest that you don't do that unless you want the rest of the Guardians tailing you today."

I considered my options. "Fine, but you don't make any comments about where we go."

He winked. "Lingerie?"

I let out an exasperated breath. "Job applications."

Mav cocked his head. "You can't do that in town?"

I rolled my eyes as I motioned for him to leave my house while I locked up. "The last thing I want is to have a job working for your Alpha."

"You know he isn't the *boss* of everything, right?"

"He sure thinks he is," I chuckled. I unlocked my little beater of a car and Mav slid into the passenger seat easily, even though he looked like he was being squeezed into a clown car. I looked at his truck parked on the side of the road and shrugged. He could have offered his ride, but a little torture wouldn't be so bad. It would keep the other Guardians from me... hopefully.

"So why are you here, exactly?" I asked as we were cruising down the interstate. I hadn't turned on the music and had waited for him to speak but he remained silent. Eventually it wore me down.

Mav raised his thick brows and leaned against the passenger door. "There have been... recent developments with the rogue wolves."

I tapped my thumbs on the steering wheel. "Recent developments that you want to share?"

He gave me a toothy grin. "Classified."

I pouted. "I don't even know you."

"Exactly why I won't be telling you classified information."

"I mean, I don't know you well enough for you to be *protecting* me. How do I know you won't try to hurt me?"

Before I knew it he was pulling his shirt from his body, I was trying to not swerve into oncoming traffic and all the while he was looking awfully smug. "What the hell are you doing?"

He jabbed a meaty finger at his chest. "This will prove to you that I am who I say I am. I took an oath to my Alpha and I will take one to you too."

I held my hand up and ignored the crest stamped into his chest. The one like Knox's. "Don't you dare do anything like that."

A rumbling laugh filled the car. "You don't want me to make an oath to you?"

"That's the last thing I want from you, any of you. All I wanted was a normal life. I want a normal life now. That is why I am applying at all of these places."

Mav pulled his shirt back over his beautifully bronzed body. "You will never be normal again."

I gritted my teeth together as I pulled into a parking space on the side of the road. The city wasn't very big but looking up at all the corporate buildings, I felt really small. "I have your Alpha to thank for that."

I slammed the door so hard the glass rattled in the door. I took a deep breath as I walked up to the first building.

CHAPTER 43
RAFE CRIMSON

Tracey watched me from the corner of the cottage. Carden was no longer chained to the wall but he was warded against leaving Granny's hut. Knox hadn't been able to breach the wards around the traitor's mind but during the full moon, it would be on.

He watched me with easy eyes. Tracey was the only one with me now. Granny couldn't stand to look at the man any longer and was staying at the Manor. "Why won't you let me leave?"

My shoulders slumped. "We have been over this countless times."

Carden rolled his eyes. "Ah, yes, you have to know who did this to me."

"Do you even know what you are?" Tracey whispered from the corner of the room.

"No, but I know one thing..." Carden's face went

grim. "They are sending an army and when they do, nothing will stop them."

Tracey pushed away from the wall and threw herself out of the cottage. I followed behind her. I couldn't listen to him say the same thing over and over again. An army? It wasn't plausible.

"Where is Jade today? Shouldn't she be at the preschool class?" I asked as soon as the door closed behind me. I took a deep breath of fresh air and followed my friend to her parent's home.

Tracey glanced at me from over her shoulder and shook her head. "No, she is applying for jobs in the city. I told Mav to go annoy her for the day."

I pinched the bridge of my nose. "Are you trying to drag her away? He will run her ragged."

Tracey shrugged. "I would never send any of the others. They're too serious for their own good. Or there's Knox who will probably try to get in her pants before they would have made it out of the city."

A growl rolled through my chest and then my fur sprouted over my arms. Tracey spun on her heel and ran at me. She punched my shoulder before my wolf could take over. "Sorry."

She rolled her eyes. "Don't. You have zero reasons to be protective over her right now."

"I could think of a few reasons,"

Tracey smacked me then. "You have *zero* reasons right now to be protective. She needs someone to watch out for her. She needs a friend, someone that will be a good friend to her. Someone that isn't me. She needs people that can relate to her."

I pressed my lips together and nodded. She was right. Mav would be the best friend she could ask for. After all, Mav had been turned against his will too.

After dropping off my resume to at least fifteen businesses, I was exhausted and not anywhere near
prepared to deal with the massive Guardian in my
front seat. Thankfully all the businesses I was going
to were in the same block and I didn't have to walk
far. Not that my wolf minded much she was itching
for a good run. It was the full moon after all and I
had no idea what to expect. All I knew was that my
wolf was going to be ecstatic.

Mav had the passenger seat leaned all the way
back and was scrolling on his phone. He didn't look
up at me as I slid back into the car. I pulled away
from the curb and didn't bother with speaking. The
sun was still high in the sky but I could feel my wolf
growing stronger. There was a restlessness inside of

my limbs that I had never experienced before. I took a shaky breath as I maneuvered my car through the traffic and back to my house.

"See, everything was fine," I didn't know if I was trying to reassure him or myself.

Mav let out a grunt and didn't say anything.

"You were awfully chatty earlier, what happened?" I didn't know why I cared. I hardly knew the man but there was that jittery feeling under my skin again and I had to do whatever it took to get it to either; go away or to calm. Talking seemed to be the only thing that would help for now.

His light eyes cut toward me. "I got reprimanded by the Alpha."

I rolled my eyes. "Tracey sent you with me?"

He grunted again.

"Your company was nice today, I think I would have been a lot more anxious had you not tagged along." I hoped that helped smooth out his wounded pride.

His eyebrow quirked up slightly. I barely caught it. "Tracey cares about you a lot and she wants you to pledge into the pack."

I snickered. "Apparently I'll die if I don't find a pack soon."

Mav's face went slack. "I don't think *you* will die if you don't pledge to an Alpha, but I guess we will all see tonight. You will feel a pull to Rafe if he's supposed to be your commanding officer."

I scoffed. "I would like to think that no one is."

Mav's lip rose in a smirk. "I have a feeling you're definitely a sigma or maybe," he grinned. "You're an Alpha and you'll put Rafe in his place."

All I could do was stare straight as I drove but there was a tad bit of satisfaction that rolled through me. It felt a little like relief.

Naked.

I was going to be naked in front of the rest of the pack. It was the one thing that was holding me back from jogging through the woods to the pack lands. It was the last thing I wanted to do. I could go the rest of my existence without showing my tits to a little community. Tracey walked out from the darkness of the trees and smiled at me.

"Don't try to talk yourself out of it."

I took a deep breath. She was wearing jogger sweatpants and a zip-up jacket. Her hair was pulled back away from her face and her eyes were glowing.

The sun had gone down just a short while before she had stepped away from the tree line and I could feel the moon pulling me. Pulling my wolf to the surface.

"I don't know if I'm ready for this," I chewed on my lip.

Tracey took my hand in hers and smiled. "I remember my first shift under the full moon. It was one of the best nights of my life."

"Really?"

"Really," She pulled me in for a bone-crushing hug and I felt a little better. "The rest of the pack will be gone by the time we get there. No one will see you naked. I don't like to shift in front of the others yet either. They don't expect me to shift with them."

That helped ease some of the anxiety. I held her hand tightly and we walked into the woods together. The smell of blood was gone, thankfully but I still couldn't get the memory of what happened to disappear from my thoughts. Tonight would also be the night that Knox took a walk through Carden's memories as a wolf. The thought didn't sit well with me.

Almost time. My wolf purred in my mind. I was somewhat excited for her. She was a quiet wolf, at least for now, and I didn't exactly know what to expect. Changed wolves went through things a little differently than the ones born with their wolves. They grew with their wolves, whereas I was just kind of forced to be with mine. Vivian had mentioned the story of the first werewolf but I had forgotten to ask about it again until now.

I stopped walking halfway to the pack lands. "Can you tell me the story of the first werewolf?"

Tracey's teeth were blinding as she smiled. "Thousands of years ago there was a boy who was valiant and courageous. His name was Ramadon. He was abandoned as a child on the full moon. A pack of wolves spared his life that night instead of eating him like they should have. There were hunters in the woods that night and they heard the howling of the wolves. The wolves led the hunters to the small child, in hopes that they would save the baby. The hunters took the baby home where the village raised him. He was truly one of a kind and loved by all. As he grew older he felt a pull to the woods. He would often run through the forest with the hunters and sometimes slip away through the night to feel the forest beneath his feet. One night the wolves ran beside him. They recognized the child they had rescued and accepted him into their pack. Secretly Ramadon ran with the wolves and hunted with them as much as he could. Ramadon befriended one wolf in particular. They would bring each other meals and fur pelts. They were practically inseparable.

One full moon there were hunters from another village prowling through the forest. Ramadon and the other wolves didn't see them until it was too late. The arrow blazed through the air but before it could pierce Ramadon in the chest, the black wolf dove in front of it to save his life. As his friend's life spilled from his body, Ramadon prayed to the gods. He swore that he would do what it took to protect the wolves, as much as the wolves had protected him. No one knows what happened after that but it was said that the goddess of life came down and merged their souls. They would be the guardians of the wolves and the humans. Ramadon would protect the humans from the wolves and eventually, the other nightmarish creatures that would come to be, and his other half would protect the wolves from the humans. That's how it has been since the beginning."

"What about his true mate?"

Tracey's eyes twinkled. "They say there was

another human that had been blessed with a wolf spirit in another village."

"Are you going to tell me the story of her?" My heart swelled. I didn't know why but the legend had opened something up inside of me. It had made me feel connected to my wolf in a new way. It gave me a connection to her that I knew I needed.

Tracey tugged on my hand and dragged me through the rest of the forest. "Maybe another time. My wolf is itching for a good run and I know she is dying to meet yours."

"Best friends for life," I muttered.

"We are going to be best friends for a lot longer than life, don't you know that we are immortal?"

She took off running and a laugh burst from my chest as I chased after her. Maybe the answers could wait. Maybe all that mattered was living in the moment tonight. My wolf surely liked that idea. Tracey unzipped her jacket as I peeled my shirt from my body and before I could blink her massive honey-colored wolf was standing in front of me. I took a deep breath again and closed my eyes as I shimmied my pants down. Before my pants hit the forest floor my wolf was surging forward. I gasped as the pops and cracks echoed off of the trees. It was different than before. Nothing hurt this time as my wolf took over and then we ran.

There were no words to describe what happened next. The feeling of my wolf taking over was interesting. She pushed forward in my consciousness and as much as I tried to hold onto the reigns, it wasn't possible.

Sorry. She muttered into my mind and I felt my worries ease away. I didn't fade completely but I let her call all the shots. It was easier, comfortable even.

Other wolves came bounding out of the woods around us and I had a momentary feeling of panic before my wolf took over once again.

I have a name. There she was again, speaking to me.

I didn't think to ask. This is all so new for me. I thought back to her.

Nalia is what I was known as in my past life. It was such an ancient powerful name and for a moment, I wanted to ask what her past life was like. Why she was with me even.

My story is for another time.

I imagined that I was reclining in the darkness, surrounded by warm fuzzies as I drifted through my consciousness. *Are all wolves from another time?*

Nalia was silent for a moment as she pounced on

Tracey's heels. *No, most of them, their spirits are born together. They are bound within the heavens. They become one.*

I let myself sink farther into my subconscious then turned it off. What kind of trouble could Nalia find in one night?

CHAPTER 45
RAFE CRIMSON

Jade's wolf was a blinding white and as she passed me up in the woods I caught sight of her eyes. They flashed between green and yellow as she ran. She looked to be lost in thought which was odd as her eyes switched back and forth. There was a desire low within me to grab ahold of the bond that had started to form between us and pull it taut to speak to her. But I couldn't force her allegiance to our pack, even if I wanted to.

There were so many things that I wanted to do but I had to be patient and it wasn't one of my virtues. So I watched as she chased Tracey through the woods and to a stream. Tracey avoided the running water, she couldn't swim very well, but Jade dove in headfirst like a happy puppy.

I sat back on my haunches and cocked my head

while she played in the stream. Mud and dirt washed out of her white coat as she shook her body. Before I knew it was running out of the water at top speed... right for me.

I held my ground and my wolf let out a growl before she hopped right over us and let out a happy yip. Her eyes were no longer switching colors but were instead a vibrant gold. Her tongue lolled out of her mouth as she circled me. I laid my head on my paws as I considered what was happening. I thought of the moments in her room a few days prior and my wolf perked up.

Her eyes had been green. They had never gone yellow. I lifted my head and pressed my snout to the side of Jade's wolf. She didn't growl, just sat back on her haunches and let me explore. A purr rumbled through her chest.

The massive white wolf smelled like Jade, but yet, she didn't. She smelled like something else.

Something ancient. My wolf whispered.

Perplexed I led the group of wolves away from the water. Tracey kept throwing me glares as the wolves would bound into the water. If I didn't do something she would try to rip my throat out. Her wolf hated water more than anything.

CHAPTER 46
JADE RIVERS

When I woke up, I was back to having control of my body and Nalia was slumbering away in my mind. She was like a mental house cat. I could practically picture her peeking open an eye to glare at me as the thought passed through.

I was naked and covered from head to toe in mud and foliage. Someone had put a blanket over my body and I could hardly feel the cold of the morning dew around me. I shivered as I sat up and then my body went ramrod straight as I realized I wasn't alone.

Nalia, you are in the dog house for this.

She mocked a yawn in my mind. *I trust our Alpha.*

Not our Alpha.

Rafe sat a few feet away from me but he was fully clothed. He wore a flannel button-down over a white t-shirt. The white shirt was tucked into his worn jeans and his feet were bare.

I raised my eyebrows at them as I pulled the blanket tighter around myself. "How long have I been sleeping?"

He tilted his head at me and his wet hair flopped over his eyes. "For about an hour. You just didn't want to stop running."

I winced as I moved my legs. They were definitely sore. The soreness that I had experienced the first day after my second shift was nothing like this. Everything felt more intense and deeper. "Nalia didn't want to stop running."

Rafe leaned back against a tree and watched me carefully. "Nalia?"

"My wolf," I nodded. My stomach growled and Rafe turned his head so I could stand to wrap the blanket around myself better. When I looked up, his eyes were on my body that was wrapped tightly in the thin blanket. Desire filled the air and it took everything inside of me to walk away from him and not climb him like a tree.

"Let's get you some breakfast, I'm sure you're starving. I don't think I've ever seen a wolf dive into the water before."

I choked on a laugh. "She did what?"

"You jumped headfirst into a stream on the west side of the pack lands."

I rubbed my hands down my arms. "Nalia is really in the dog house for this."

Rafe held his hand out to stop me. "What do you mean?"

I got the distinct impression I had said the wrong thing. I didn't get the chance to explain as the rest of the Guardians seemed to come out of the forest around us. They all had a similar build, freaking huge, rippling muscles, while they were each different heights. Knox was easily the tallest, then Mav. The rest I hadn't learned their names yet but I could recognize their scents from the night before. There was a growl from Rafe before the Guardians held their hands up and took a step back. I lifted my lip in a snarl. Why was he acting this way?

It took me only a second to realize that they weren't looking at my face but instead my body wrapped in the thin blanket. I rolled my eyes. My wolf laughed in my head.

"You're all stupid," I shoved through the muscle barrier in front of me and prowled to the Manor. *Way too much testosterone.* "You all get naked then transform into wolves in front of each other but here

I am, half-naked and you all lose your senses?" I groaned. I hated men.

Since I was a child, I had never known stress. I had never had a need to know it. My parents hovered and always provided me with what I needed. As I grew older and they started to travel, things weren't as easy, but not stressful. But as the days go by and my wolf tries to come to the surface more times than not, I am saddled with a difficult task.

Find a job and responsibility or continue to put my family in danger. Even though my parents love to travel, they will always come back. They will never leave my side and if I don't put some distance between us... they will get hurt.

I pace my kitchen in frustration as I wait for my steak to cook on the stove. I no longer crave raw meat like I once had and my senses were starting to straighten out a bit. I run my hands down the front of my shirt as I consider calling Tracey. It had been a few days since the full moon and a few days since I had delivered all of my resumes too. My wolf stayed slumbering inside of my mind, only offering advice when she wanted to, not when I actually need it.

Sizzling and popping from the stove brought me back to the present and what was happening. A knock at the door sounded a few seconds after my phone pinged an alert to someone walking up the driveway. That person was absolutely the last one I want to see. I would have preferred Rafe over him, and that was saying something. I clicked the stove off and removed the pan from the hot burner before I went to answer the door. Just because I can stomach cooked meat doesn't mean that I like it well done.

Knox was waiting on the other side of the door. A brown paper bag was clutched in one hand, and something indistinguishable in the other. When I open the door he offered me a timid smile. I crossed my arms over my chest and lift an eyebrow in contempt.

"What can I do for you?"

He shifted from one foot to the other at the tone of my voice. I don't blame him for his anxiety, I was far from friendly. I still don't like him and the way he tore through that man in the woods. Though it was effective, it was also terrifying. I still see it in my nightmares, except he's ripping my heart out instead of the stranger's. I took a long sniff and identify Chinese takeout in the brown bag and a DVD in his other hand. A peace offering, maybe?

"Rafe sent me on patrol tonight but it's cold and my wolf hates getting wet," He shivered for extra measure then smiled at me again. He looked so innocent that I could almost forget that his hands were made to kill, that he was forged to murder for his Pack.

I eased back a step, but only slightly. I narrowed my eyes as I considered his words. "None of the other patrols have been sent into my yard. What is going on?"

Knox shook out his shoulders, for extra emphasis on his wolf hating the cold before I step aside. "None of the patrols have gotten this close to your house because the rogues had stayed away. They have gotten closer and closer to this house and Rafe is worried."

My eyebrows inched up my forehead. So that explained the smell every time I left my house yesterday. Something smelled off- *wrong*- when I would leave. Especially around my car, but Rafe was adamant on the fact that I didn't need to go anywhere without a guard. I had waved off his paranoia and not listened but now, I didn't mind as much, even if it was this lunatic. Knox closed the door behind him as I went back to the kitchen. I pulled potato salad from the fridge and leftover grilled vegetables from the microwave. I appreciated the peace offering of takeout but I wasn't so easily bought. I ignored the Guardian as I prepared my plate. Knox didn't say anything as he searched the drawers for a fork and dug into the first cardboard container. It was sweet and sour chicken, it had once been a favorite of mine. Did he know this from Tracey or was he just getting the basics? Who didn't like sweet and sour chicken? I speared the grilled asparagus on my plate and watched the man leaning against the counter. Tonight he wore jeans and a tight white t-shirt, his auburn hair was pushed away from his face. From what I could tell, his wolf wasn't close tonight. Instead of the yellow hue his eyes usually were, they were a navy blue tonight.

"Have you made any progress with Carden?" I absolutely hated saying his name. Not only did it hurt my heart but it also made me feel guilty.

Knox cracked his neck and nodded slowly as he took another bite of his chicken. "Yes, though I have never seen these wolves or witches before. I thought it would have been easy discovering their identity, but so far, it's been harder."

An idea occurred to me. "Maybe I could help?"

Knox grinned around his fork. "That's the best

thing I have heard all day and honestly, it would bother the hell out of Rafe."

I rolled my eyes, though I did like the sound of that. Bothering Rafe didn't sound like a bad thing. "Then, I'm in."

Knox looked me over and then a devilish grin replaced the other one. "There are many ways we could annoy Rafe."

Maybe Knox wasn't such a bad escort after all.

CHAPTER 47

Knox was starting to become a bright light in my very anxious life. I was going back to classes now at the University and having his presence every morning made me feel calm. The first time he had picked me up from school, his idea- not mine, Rafe had a fit. Tracey told me he stewed in the woods for hours. Apparently, Knox hadn't been the one sent on babysitting duty, it was Mav. Which didn't make sense as he had been in trouble for going against Alpha orders before. I wasn't sure what was happening behind the scenes with all of them but it was giving me a headache.

I clenched and unclenched my hands as I walked to my last class of the day. My wolf hardly cared about coming out to see what was happening in the real world unless we were going for a run, but even that didn't seem to excite her like it did on the full moon. Which was a good thing, it meant I could go back to school and live a normal life. Or as normal as I could get it while having a wolf living inside of my mind and body.

When I slid into my seat at the back of the room, I smelled it again. That wrongness in the air. My hackles rose as I looked around me. Everyone was faced forward getting ready for the lecture but I couldn't move. I was frozen in place. Nalia rose to the surface in my mind and a growl tried to rumble through my chest. I swallowed it back and clutched my shaking hands under my desk. I wiggled my fingers as fur rolled across the tops of my hands. My lips trembled as I exhaled.

This was very bad. When I finally looked up, the hair on the back of my neck stood up to attention. The feeling of being watched was overwhelming. I folded my hands together and looked beside me. The boy sitting there couldn't have been my age. He looked young, like too young to be in college. His facial hair was spotty on his face and his limbs looked too long for his body shape. But those weren't the things that kept my attention on him. It was the way his head cocked toward mine, in a predatory manner. When his eyes met mine, they shifted to gold.

The professor had entered the room and was getting set up on the floor. The projector clicked on. I inched to the edge of my seat but Nalia kept me from bolting.

Do not run. He likes the scent of fear. He's baiting you.

I swallowed hard and pulled my phone in front of me. This professor was more strict about cellphone usage but thankfully, with the projector on, he wouldn't see me back in the corner. I sent out a quick text to Knox. His reply was lighting fast. I was actually surprised he didn't jump into the room to interrupt the lecture.

Do not engage. He could just be a rogue reacting to the smell of your pheromones. We have no war with the rogues as long as they stay away from pack lands. I will be waiting in the hall for you.

That eased some of my worries, but not all of it. The rogue seated close to me kept his eyes on me the entire lecture and didn't even take notes. How the professor didn't jump down his throat was beyond me. He was usually quick to catch those things. He hated students that didn't pay attention or take notes. I knew better than the rest, I had been caught on my first day in his class, not paying attention. The tongue lashing in front of the rest of the students was humiliating and reminded me of high school. None of my other professors cared at all about what we did, except cheating.

When the professor announced dismissal I was careful to push my chair in slowly and walk carefully out of the room. I hated giving the wolf my back and Nalia practically shouted in my mind about it, but the human world was oblivious to wolves. I couldn't face off with the gangly boy in the middle of the room. I would have to turn my back on him to at least get him away from the humans. They wouldn't be safe if the rogue went off the walls crazy. Most of them were insane because they didn't have an Alpha to pledge to. *Is that what I would become?*

Knox was leaning against the white cinderblock walls when I came out of the room. His dark red hair was a mess around his head and his navy eyes were now bright gold. Knox wrinkled his nose in disgust. "You need to shower. You smell like him."

"How?" I lifted my arm to sniff myself and sure enough, I did. I fought back a gag.

Knox snarled as he placed his hand on my lower back and led me out of the school. I didn't miss the appreciative glances thrown his way as he slipped his sunglasses over his nose. I also didn't miss the sneers as they watched his hand on my lower back. The gangly rogue that had been beside me in the classroom was now gone. He hadn't emerged behind me. He had disappeared.

"I think he rubbed his scent all over your chair. He's baiting us but I can't figure out why." Knox ran his hand down his face. I felt the pebbling of fur ripple across my arms again. He stiffened beside me as he felt it. "You need to keep your wolf in check, Jade."

"I'm trying," My voice came out in a growling mess. Knox bristled as he opened my car door for me then slipped into the driver seat.

He flipped the AC on to full blast and I felt my wolf relax. Nalia wasn't happy but she wouldn't force a shift in the car, at least not right now. My shoulders relaxed as I leaned back in my seat.

"When was the last time you had some fun?" Knox's voice took on a different tone and it was like the last hour hadn't happened. He seemed to be more relaxed as he wove through the traffic to get us home. When he missed the exit for the pack lands, I was confused.

I wrinkled my eyebrows as I tried to not think of

the night Carden tried to claim me. "It's been a hot second."

Knox cocked his head toward me and mischief twisted his lips. "I think you need to get out of the house, Jade. All of this stress isn't good for your wolf and neither is all of this rogue mess. She is going to lash out and I would hate for it to happen in the grocery store."

I wanted to deny what he was saying but Nalia was eerily silent. She was agreeing with him, without openly agreeing with him. I sighed. "I'm not going to another party if that's what you have planned."

Me and parties no longer mixed. Even though I really wanted them to be normal to me again, they never would. I would never be able to enjoy the party lifestyle that I had been so used to, the lifestyle that I had loved at one point. Knox shook his head as he pulled into my driveway. This time my parents were watching.

My phone rang after exactly a minute. "Hello?"

Much to my surprise, it was my mother on the other end. "Is someone visiting the house? I haven't seen that car before."

My lips pinched together to keep myself from

laughing. "Yes, I've been carpooling to and from school with one of my friends."

"That isn't Tracey's car," My dad's voice was slightly stern. Knox leaned against the door and an easy grin spread across his lips. I shoved my door open, not giving him the opportunity for him to get out and get my door for me. That was the *last* thing my parents needed to see. It would only egg them on. I unlocked the door and Knox followed behind me with a slow swagger. He knew they were watching and he was going to put on a show. I gritted my teeth together as I shook my head at him. The audacity.

"No," I dragged the word out slightly. There was nothing to feel guilty over... except I had to lie to them again and it wasn't anything scandalous. "It isn't Tracey's car."

"You brought a boy into the house," My mom actually whispered this like she knew Knox had super hearing or something. He grinned across the kitchen at me.

"Yes, I did." I didn't know how I was going to play this out. "We aren't seeing each other in case you're wondering."

My dad grumbled something I couldn't hear. My mom didn't sound as chipper as before when she finally turned back to the phone. "Well, that's disappointing."

I choked on the water I had been sipping on. I didn't think it was possible, but Knox's grin only continued to grow bigger. Lord help me. I let out an exasperated sound. "What does that mean?"

"I mean you have brought home some very *fine* male specimens as of late, and honestly," She paused and I knew it was because she was walking away from dad. "I'm not mad about it. *Whew*, he is probably the best looking so far."

I set the water bottle down on the counter. There was no way I was going to be able to drink anything while on the phone with her. This time I didn't even look at the werewolf in my kitchen. I turned on my heel and marched up the stairs. "Mom!"

She laughed and it released some tension in my shoulders. "I mean, you know it's true."

"Knox is just my friend."

She let out a choked sound and I knew this conversation had to be over. "He even has a hot name."

"I hope you're enjoying your trip! I really need to take a shower." But then I realized I said the wrong thing as I listened to my parents grapple with the phone.

"Don't do anything I wouldn't do!" My mom shouted as my dad grumbled something again.

"Not happening like that! Goodbye!" I practically threw the phone onto my bed as I scrubbed my hands down my face.

"It could though," Knox's voice behind me made me jump but instead of away from him, I jumped toward him and all wolf instincts took over. I swung at his face and he ducked it easily. "But you still smell like the rogue. Maybe I'll join you after his scent is gone."

I bit the inside of my cheek and slammed the door in his face. "Are all wolves arrogant like this?"

CHAPTER 48
RAFE CRIMSON

"Absolutely not," I growled at my best friend. Knox had returned to the pack lands after he checked the perimeter of Jade's house when she was tucked in bed. My patrol shift was about to start even though my Guardians didn't like that at all. They preferred to be the ones on the front line, especially with how many rogues seemed to be prowling around our town. There had never been so many. I didn't know where they could be coming from.

Mav leaned against the wall and shook his head. "Knox is right, her anxiety and stress are high. I went with her to the store the other day. Jade needs some stress relief."

I pressed my tongue to the inside of my cheek and looked back at Knox. I knew he would tread carefully but he had the highest body count out of all of us. He would pursue her even if they weren't mates. "Is your idea of stress relief what I think it is?"

Knox ran his tongue over his teeth as he lifted an eyebrow. "If that's what you need from me, Alpha."

It took every ounce of willpower in my body to not launch myself at him and rip the smirk from his face. I took a deep breath and paced across the room instead. "Does anyone else have a better idea?"

Mav's lips pulled away from his teeth in a timid smile. "Maybe we could take her downtown."

Between him and Knox, they knew her better than I did. Which was my fault. I could have gotten to know her better, but I apparently had my head stuck in my ass, as Tracey said. "Why would you do that?"

Knox shrugged his massive shoulders. "She liked to party, right? She told me the last thing she wanted to do was party but maybe some karaoke would do her some good."

It was Tracey's turn to put forth input. "And who would bring her? Last time the guys went downtown for karaoke, there were several bar fights and none of you can sing to save your life."

Knox rolled his eyes. "You must be tone-deaf. My voice is magical."

Tracey snorted. "It's *you* that is tone-deaf."

"Tracey is right," I ran my hands through my hair. "If you take her downtown, you aren't allowed to get rowdy."

Mav looked disappointed and Knox looked entirely too smug. "We aren't going downtown without you, Alpha." That was why Knox looked smug and Mav looked disappointed. My best friend broke away from the wall as he continued to speak. "You want her to swear to our pack before the rogues get her, you'll have to go with us."

I crossed my arms over my chest and looked to Tracey for some help. She shook her head. She wasn't going to get in the middle of this.

"Fine, but I'm not wearing matching outfits with the rest of you." I knew my words were useless as Mav grinned.

CHAPTER 49
JADE RIVERS

Nalia wanted me to get out of bed but that was the last thing I wanted to do. The semester was almost over and the classes I had for the day weren't entirely important. I had hardly slept the night before and even though the sun was shining into my bedroom, all I wanted to do was go back to sleep.

You need to get up.

This was the first time she had interrupted my want to sleep in. Since when did she care? All I did was yank the covers higher over my head. Maybe she would get the hint then.

The Guardians are going to pull you from your bed.

"They're going to get the fight of their lives then," I muttered back.

When Nalia realized her efforts were futile, she slipped back to the corner of my mind to sleep herself. She wanted to act like she was well-rested but she was just as stressed as I was. She bristled and flew to the surface at any random noise. She was ready to protect us, no matter the cost. All night we had done that. The AC had kicked on loudly and she had practically burst from my skin.

When one of the Guardians entered the perimeter of my yard, I kicked the blankets from me and dragged myself to the shower. As I scrubbed my hair I thought of all the places I had sent my resume to. I wondered if I could call them. Maybe this was silly and I just needed to get a job waiting tables somewhere. That was what a lot of the girls around town did. There were enough restaurants in this college town. I leaned my head against the cool tile and took a deep breath as I considered my options. My parents would never consider that a real job. They would only accept an office position or they would never leave me alone about it. They knew how expensive it was to live in this town and I would have to work probably two jobs in order to keep my head above water. I needed an internship for my degree and graduation was right around the corner.

When someone knocked on the door, Nalia was ready. My claws exploded from my fingers and a growl echoed around the little bathroom.

"Hey, it's me," Tracey's voice squeaked on the other side of the door. I knew one of the Guardians was here and waiting for me to get to school but I had been too lost in my own thoughts to realize that my friend was with them. I could have concentrated on my hearing and known she was with them. I could have used my sense of smell and identified her immediately but between me and my wolf, we were on edge.

I shook my hands out but the claws stayed. Finally I gave up and dried myself off, claws and all. I wrapped the towel around myself. My hands trembled as I opened the bathroom door. Tracey was seated on my bed, with her backpack on the floor. Her bright eyes were filled with concern then worry as they took in my claws.

"Are you scared living here by yourself?"

I shook my head. That was the last thing I was afraid of. "No, I just have a lot on my mind."

Tracey leaned back on my pillows. "Do you wanna talk about it?"

"How do I get these to go away?" I held my hands up and Nalia sighed in my head.

Sorry, I'll let go now.

Just like that, the claws were gone and my fingers

were back to normal. Tracey frowned. "Tell me what's going on in that pretty head of yours."

"I'm not afraid of being here alone, I'm afraid of being here when my parents get back. I feel like I'm putting them in danger because I can't control what is happening in my life." I dug through my dresser to keep my hands busy.

"That's why you applied to all those internships," Tracey muttered behind me.

All I could do was nod my head as I pulled out a pair of jeans and a sweater. Even though I'm not cold, keeping up appearances is important when the temperature outside has dropped. Tracey is all bundled up and I know she wasn't cold either. "Yeah, but none of them have called me back and my parents will eventually come home. It'll probably be sooner rather than later."

"Why do you think that?" The bed let out a squeak as Tracey moved.

I don't worry about privacy as I drop my towel and get dressed. She's seen me nude enough times and I know she isn't weird about it either. "Because they caught Knox on the camera. Now my dad is going to get super protective and my mom will be all up in it like she's living vicariously through me."

Tracey snickered and I finally turned around.

She's perched the edge of the bed and looking at her hands. "We might have some jobs around the pack lands that you could apply for. We closed down a lot because of the rogues and what's going on with Carden, but there are always behind the scenes positions open."

My shoulders fell as I sighed. It could solve all of my problems but... "I would say yes, but I want to get a job because of my value, not because of being a wolf or being your friend."

Tracey nodded her head like she knew that's what I was going to say. "I can keep an eye open for you and send you job listings if you'd like."

I accept it because I know I have no other options. When my parents get home, I need to have a game plan.

Because we skipped school, Tracey dragged me to the pack lands. She starts with using the excuse of the Guardians being tired or something silly like that. If Knox heard her say that about him, he would be entirely too upset. He would possibly never admit defeat or exhaustion. I had seen him jog down my road a few times. The first time I had seen him, he told me he had run twelve miles. He wasn't even sweating.

When I open the car door I could feel the shift in the air. Something exciting was happening. There was a buzz in the air that hadn't been there as long as I had been a wolf. I looked at Tracey with suspicion and she shrugged innocently.

I kicked her door closed as someone cleared their throat behind me. When I turned around Alice, Rafe's mother, was standing there.

"It's been too long since you've been back to the pack!" She exclaimed excitedly. Her dark hair was pulled back from her face in a tight braid and she wore dark jeans and a tank top tucked into it.

No need to pretend here. I thought to myself.

"Hi, Alice, I have missed seeing some of the faces around here." And a voice in my head interrupted to say *especially one in particular.* This time I couldn't tell if it was Nalia or myself. I ignored it. After a few seconds, I found myself looking for Rafe. He was usually the first one to come out and give me a hard time when I would get to the pack lands but today he was nowhere to be found. I had to fight to keep the frown from my lips.

As if Alice could read my thoughts she smiled.

"Rafe had some pack business elsewhere for the day."

I nodded my head like that wasn't what I was thinking but the blush spreading across my cheeks gave me away. I was about to dart away when her hand touched my elbow. "Can we speak for a moment?"

Worry ran down my insides but I tried to cool it before Nalia freaked out again. That was the last thing I needed to happen. "What's up?"

"I was wondering if you were still looking for a job," Alice grinned at me and the worry I felt a second ago amped up a notch. Tracey raised her hands behind Alice and shook her head before she mouthed, *I had nothing to do with this.*

I bit the inside of my cheek. I was but I didn't want to admit it to her. I still had the same reasoning I had given Tracey flitting through my head. "Um,"

Alice took a step back as if she could smell my anxiety. Then it hit me, she could smell it. I just wasn't in touch with my wolf enough to realize it.

We could smell their emotions too, if you'd let me. There she was.

"I told Tracey I didn't want any help with that. I know you all mean well, but..." I trailed off, unsure of how to continue.

Alice frowned this time. "Tracey didn't have anything to do with this. I'm confused. You did drop your resume off at our headquarters downtown, didn't you?"

My eyebrows pulled together. "Did Rafe know I went downtown and intercept it?"

Alice laughed and shook her head. "No, Rafe probably wouldn't like it very much if he knew I was offering this to you, actually."

A bit of satisfaction flickered through me at that.

She's telling the truth. Nalia confirmed in my head.

"We are in need of an accountant but not at our downtown location. We need someone here, at the Manor, to help with all of that." She put her hand on my arm and led me into the Manor before us. I didn't know what to say.

"Wait, what is your headquarters called?"

Alice opened the door for us and motioned me to follow her. Down the hall behind the stairs is a massive office. In the left corner, there was a massive dark wood desk that held two Mac monitors and a filing cabinet underneath it. There were two folders spread out on the desk. "CP Industries." The bright red CP flash through my memory and I want to kick myself for not putting it together sooner. "That's more of our international sector that deals with other packs in other countries. We are a lot more than we seem here, Jade."

She opened the first folder and handed me the first page. Listed down it were businesses in bold that the Crimson Pack owns and operates. "As you can see, we need more help than what we have."

I nodded my head as I looked over the numbers and all of the names. The library, the fire station, grocery stores, gas stations. I blinked slowly and put the paper on the desk.

"I would hate to shoot myself in the foot but I'm not sure I'm qualified for this position."

Alice walked around the desk and sat in the plush black velvet chair there. It looked brand new. "You are more than qualified for this position. It doesn't require much." She slid the second folder toward me. "In this one, you will see your salary as well as an agreement for you to live here on the property."

It's like she wrapped up all my fears and insecurities and fixed them all with a big fat bow on top. When I opened the folder, I couldn't help but let it slip from my fingers. The number was entirely too high and they're letting me live on the pack lands without being a pack member? *This is too good to be true.*

"I'm not a member of your pack." The words tumbled out of my lips before I could stop them.

Alice only smiled. "Well, the first has to do with you being a Sigma, which I had no idea before. You won't ever have to pledge to a pack unless your wolf needs it. There are many benefits to pledging forth but I can understand your hesitation. More than anyone else, I wish I could understand why my son does the things he does, but unfortunately, I can't see into his mind. I trust you, as does the rest of the pack. You have a place here. A place you can run free and not have to worry about shifting, as well as enough money to pay for the rest of your degree and some extras."

Why hadn't anyone told me I was a Sigma? How did she even know? Was it all another guess? Did I even want to bring it up with the rest of this bizarre interview?

I swallowed thickly before I could answer. "I don't need charity." Something iced over in her gaze. "This isn't charity. I know your parents have money. I know you are used to getting mostly everything you have and not having to work for it." She leaned back in the chair and steepled her fingers together. She was a businesswoman now. "I require hard work, but I know you can provide it and the home I will provide you with, as stated in the contract, hasn't seen a good day in ages. I do take care of my own, but I don't do it out of the kindness of my heart. I require effort around here. Unfortunately for us but fortunately for you, we haven't had an accountant in ages. I've been doing most of it around here, but I don't have the schooling background. The kids around here don't want to go to college and would rather leave for work or just be lazy. The last accountant was my husband and you know he is no longer with us."

I nodded my head. This is what I wanted. I wanted to be taken seriously for my skills, for what I had to offer to a team. I blinked back the moisture in my eyes as the businesswoman in front of me melted away.

"So what do you think?"

The smile spread across my lips before I could stop it. "I think I would be stupid to say no."

"I think you're going to fit right in around here."

CHAPTER 50

RAFE CRIMSON

The stupid errand my mother had sent me on had been a dud. There were no rogues on the other side of the town, even if the scent was slightly there. She had lied without lying. She was the best at it. She knew how to manipulate the truth to her advantage. It was why my father had been so intrigued by her when they first met. It was what kept him from walking away when he preferred blondes over brunettes.

It wasn't until I returned to the Manor and heard typing in the office down the hall that I knew the reason for the trip. She had given father's job to someone. She had interviewed them without my leave. A growl rumbled down my throat. She had probably brought a human here and she knew things were strained. The last thing we needed was a human lurking around. But then the scent hit me and I knew the damage that my mother had brought down. Sitting behind my father's computer was Jade Rivers. She didn't bother to look at me as she typed away.

"What are you doing in here?" My voice sounded harsh even for my ears.

She didn't bother to look up. She kept typing away as one of her hands slid a folder to me across the desk. I opened it up and then closed it slowly. The number in there was for someone with a degree, not- not Jade. I blinked as I tried to get my thoughts together but I couldn't.

My mother was waiting for me in the kitchen. I clenched and unclenched my jaw. "You had no right."

My mother rolled her eyes. "You have no right. You are the Alpha, yet you know nothing about business. I have to do what I have to do in order to keep money flowing to our people. What would you have me do?"

I crossed my arms over my chest to hide how hard I was shaking, "How about you don't meddle?"

Her laughter was diabolical but her words weren't. "She applied at our HQ downtown. I came across the resume in my email. I didn't even know it was her for a second. She is qualified for the position."

Guilt ran down my spine and left a bad taste in my mouth. "She's going to be living in Gran's old cabin?"

The amusement that had been in my mother's eyes was now gone. "Your Gran has been gone for a long time. You know that little cabin didn't offer her much."

I shook my head. That wasn't the point. "What if she comes back?"

"There are ten bedrooms in this Manor. You act like we couldn't make room." My mother placed both of her hands on the island and leaned forward. "Don't make this harder than it needs to be. What about Jade? What about what she needs?"

Something broke inside of me at that. "She won't pledge to our pack. She needs nothing from us."

Mom shoved off of the counter and marched to where I stood. "Don't start all of that. You are the one that forced her to be a part of all of this. If you could have kept yourself from doing that, then you wouldn't be dealing with all of this."

The crack inside of my heart started to grow. There was going to be a gaping hole soon enough. "She was going to die."

Her shoulders drooped and she wrapped her arms around my waist. She was a good foot shorter than me. "Oh, honey. Sometimes things are meant that way. We can't prevent everyone from dying before we think it's their time."

"Would you have me die too, then?"

CHAPTER 51

JADE RIVERS

After three days of going over everything in the Crimson Manor's computer system, I felt like things were off to a good start. Alice Crimson had done a good job in the place of her husband over the years but I didn't know how I could possibly accept the amount of money they were offering me, especially since some days I wouldn't be working. I would go over documents, analyze budgets but then what would I do for the rest of the day? Alice had to leave on official pack business and the contract didn't state whether or not I was working full-time.

I leaned back in the velvet chair and looked at the empty space around me. Alice had said that I was allowed to decorate it any way I wanted and with my salary, the budget was large. I closed my eyes and spun around.

"Uh hem," I knew it was Rafe before I opened my eyes. I could smell him all the way from here. Pine and whiskey. My two favorite things before my life went to shit. "Are you okay?"

I nodded and went back to the computer. Did I need to look like I was busy? Technically Rafe was my boss too.

"Ya know that you don't have to be here all day, right?" I didn't even bother with looking at him. What was the point? I had heard what he had to say until he had stormed out of the house. I had felt the animosity coming off of him in waves as he realized that I was the one his mother hired to take his father's place.

"I didn't know how many hours your mother wanted me to work. The amount of money she is paying me would suggest that I am to be here twenty-four-seven."

"You only need to be here when you're doing work and if you want to bring it home with you, that's okay too."

I looked at the two monitors in front of me and wrinkled my nose. Yeah, that sounded easy enough. He laughed at my expression and walked around me. His scent wrapped around me and this time it made me dizzy as he bent over beside me. He was just a few inches from me but I couldn't breathe. I was scared of what I would do if I inhaled his scent again. Since when was it this heavenly? I had been this close to him before, hadn't I? A click sounded before he yanked open the bottom drawer on the filing cabinet.

"Mom upgraded all of our software and everything last year and she thought she needed a laptop. Everything is all synched so you don't have to do anything but find your work and do it from home if you wish." He placed the MacBook Pro on the desk beside me before he retreated to the other side of the office again.

"All you had to do was tell me you didn't want me here, I would have found a way to work around your schedule." I shrugged my shoulders like my heart didn't hurt. Like all of this wasn't hurting me, but my throat felt thick and my eyes burned. I swiped the laptop off of the table and stormed from the building. I didn't need his excuses or his wonderful scent. All I needed was the job and I could now do it without having to see him.

Tracey was reclining on my bed when I got home. I tried to not throw that laptop at her as I collapsed into the office chair in my room. "What a surprise."

"We are going out tonight," Tracey grinned and sat up from my bed.

I rolled my eyes. "I have work I need to do."

"Rafe will let you get away with one night off, it's Fridayyyyyy." She dragged the word out while she flipped over on my bed. Her curly hair hung from the side and brushed the ground.

I groaned. The idea of going out did sound nice, but I didn't want to go to a party. I would have to set ground rules or I wouldn't feel comfortable. "What do you have in mind, because I am not going to any parties around here."

Tracey smirked. "We are going downtown. No more house parties."

"So clubbing instead?" I didn't know if I liked that either but I did like the idea of getting out of the house.

All Tracey could do was wink as I disappeared into the bathroom. I looked at myself and sighed. I looked sad and worn out. There were fading bruises under my eyes from all the sleep I had lost and my cheeks were somewhat gaunt from not eating as much as I needed to.

I leaned against the counter before I splashed cold water on my face. It did nothing to help perk me up.

You should go. I think we both need it.

Nalia was right. We did need it. Even if it meant dancing till my feet hurt. I hoped it also meant lots of laughter. I didn't want to worry about boys and wanted to spend time with my best friend. I yanked the door open and leaned in the doorframe. "Fine, but I don't want to pick out my outfit. I want you to get me ready."

Tracey jumped from the bed and squealed. "This is gonna be the best night ever!"

Tornado Tracey touched down in my room approximately five minutes after that. She left clothes, shoes, and makeup in her wake. When she grabbed my shoulders and shoved me back into my chair, I started to worry about the monster I had unleashed upon myself. There was a little black dress draped across the bed in front of me and some strappy red heels on the floor. Tracey yanked my hair this way and that way and I had zero say in what was happening to my body. What was wrong with me?

By the time she was finished with my hair, my scalp was sore and I could feel tears building behind my eyes. I had never been considered tender-headed but she had delivered pain I wasn't expecting. When she turned me around to face the mirror behind my desk, I gasped. She hadn't put much makeup on me but what she did put made my green eyes glow. My hair was curled around my head in loose waves. I didn't even recognize myself. When was the last time I had actually fixed my hair and makeup? I couldn't remember the last time. I felt like a new person.

I took a deep breath as I pulled my phone out of my pocket. Maybe I was a new person now and this new person needed to grow a pair. My mom answered on the first ring.

"Hey! How's Knox doing?"

I groaned. "I am not answering that question."

"Good because I would rather talk about anything but the men in your life. At one point, you always promised I would be the only man in your life," my father's voice took over the phone.

"That sounds really lonely dad," I didn't mean for it to sound as harsh as it came out. "I have news though and I couldn't wait to share it will you both."

"If this is a preg-"

I pressed my palms into my eyes. "Don't even finish the sentence."

"Out with it!" Mom's voice went excited really quick.

"I was offered a job with the Crimson family as an accountant." My mom let out a squeal and my father let out some relief in a heavy sigh.

"What does this mean?" The seriousness has come back.

"Well, I figured it was time for me to start looking for a big girl job and possibly even getting my own place to live."

My mom gasped and my dad remained quiet. "Have we done something?"

"No, I just feel like it's time I grow up. I'll be graduating soon and I need some experience under my belt. I had originally only been looking for internships but Alice Crimson saw something in me."

Something like pride rang through my father's voice. "I like the Crimson's and I think this will be a good opportunity for you. I am so proud of you."

Tracey mouthed for me to hang up. She was right, if this phone call got any mushier, I was going to ruin my makeup. I always knew my parents were proud of me, but hearing it changed everything.

CHAPTER 52
JADE RIVERS

Tracey informed me in the car that the boys would be going with us. I didn't worry about asking which boys because I knew we would be tailed by the Guardians and I was too worried that the list would include Rafe. I didn't really look forward to seeing him again after leaving the pack lands.

Surprisingly, we arrived at the little bar before the boys did. It gave me the chance to take a deep breath and focus on our surroundings. The bar was owned by someone in the pack and most everyone that frequented it was of supernatural origins. I didn't know how I felt about possibly coming face to face with a vampire, but we would cross that bridge when we got there.

Tracey chose a corner booth before she went to order a drink at the bar. I asked for a water before she disappeared. I checked my phone for a call from my parents before I tucked it into the pocket of my dress, right beside my ID. Even though Tracey had informed me I didn't need it, I felt more comfortable having it with me.

Knox was the first one to walk through the entrance and when I caught sight of what he was wearing I about fell over. His red hair was slicked back and he wore a Hawaiian button-down shirt. But those things weren't what had me falling over. It was the jorts. The jean shorts that were cut off more than six inches above his knees. There was something sexy but also hilarious about them. The shorts showed off his muscular thighs and my mouth went dry. Was there a dress code that we missed?

Mav came in next with a swagger in his step. He leaned to the side and swung his body around as he walked right through the door. He was also wearing the ridiculous getup that Knox had on. Knox met Tracey at the bar and I watched as his eyes looked her up and down before he smirked. I raised my eyebrows and watched their flirty banter unfold. Tracey smacked him on the arm before she marched back to our spot.

Tonight her tight curls were pulled back into a bun on the top of her head and massive gold hoops swung from her ears. She wore a bodysuit that hugged all of her curves wonderfully. The army green color of it made her skin tone glow. Knox's tongue ran across his top lip as he watched her go.

"I think he baited you on purpose," I smirked as she slid into the booth beside me. "He wanted to see you walk away."

She rolled her light eyes. "He's just a flirt. He loves a good chase. If I chased back he would get scared."

"Don't let him hear you say that," Mav leaned against the top of the booth and threw us both a show-stopping smile.

Tracey pouted. "I hope he heard it. He wouldn't be able to handle a strong woman even if he wanted to."

My eyes stayed glued to the door as the other Guardians filed into the bar. Archer, Duncan, and Gabriel all wore the same thing as the other Guardians. They each had on a different colored shirt though. It looked like a cult gone wrong. Was Rafe going to be matching with them? I doubted it. He didn't seem like the type. Archer stopped at the door and pushed it back open before he peered out. His hair was the color of midnight and was cropped close to his scalp. It was a stark contrast to his pale skin. He reached out the door and grabbed a hold of something.

It took me a second to realize it was Rafe. I snorted and about fell right out of the booth. He *was* matching the other guys. What had they done to get him into his jorts?

My eyes followed the line of muscle up his thick, bronzed thighs and I wasn't mad at all about it. His green shirt with pink flowers was tucked into the worn cut-offs and every worry I had about seeing him went flying out the window. His jaw was clenched as he looked over the dimly lit room. He looked everywhere but our table.

A hand seized my wrist and yanked me over. Mav whistled low. "Damn girl, I need to see the whole outfit."

My teeth worried my bottom lip as I let the Guardian pull me from the booth and spin me around. He whistled again and I couldn't stop the giggle that escaped my lips. He knew how to flatter a girl, that was for sure. My eyes left the hulking man in front of me and searched out the Alpha. He was at the bar, gulping down the contents of his drink, all the while his eyes followed the curves of my body. My eyes strayed to the column of his throat and I felt hot desire pool low in my belly.

Mav took a step closer to me and wrapped one of my curls around his finger. His breath tickled the outside of my ear as he whispered. "Eventually, you're going to have to give in."

My eyes flicked up to his in confusion. "I don't know what you're talking about."

He licked his bottom lip. "Keep telling yourself that. Are you going to be disappointed when he doesn't come over here?"

A frown pulled at my lips. "Why wouldn't he?"

Knox's breath washed over the back of my neck. "Because he would rather not be seen with us when we get *rowdy*."

I snorted. "Too bad that he's matching all of you. He can't get out of this that easy."

Knox's hands found my waist and in a panic I looked over at Tracey. She leaned back in the booth and held her glass up in salute. *Play along.* She mouthed.

I didn't know what I was doing but I let my head fall back and rest on Knox's shoulder while Mav pulled us both to the dance floor. I didn't know what they had planned but I wasn't going to complain. Being sandwiched between two hot men wasn't a bad thing. But judging by the hairs standing up on the back of my neck, it wasn't a good thing either. I wanted to look over my shoulder and see if he was watching like I knew he was, but I couldn't. I wouldn't.

The game I was playing turned sour really quick. I was pressed between two hotties but before I knew it I was on the karaoke stage with a microphone in my hand. I shook my head as I tried to give the damned thing back to Mav but all he did was grab one for himself and pick a song on the laptop perched on a barstool. This was very bad. Tracey held her glass up again from across the room and I hoped my look was enough to scare her. Judging by her laugh, it wasn't.

CHAPTER 53
JADE RIVERS

"I don't even do this when I'm drunk. I haven't even had a taste of alcohol yet." My protesting bounced off of them.

Mav waggled his finger at me. "We have to have fun and the only way we can do that is if we get Alpha drunk enough. Seeing you up here in this tight little number will do him in. Now let's just hope you can actually sing."

I swallowed hard. The only singing I did was in the shower. This was going to go south, and fast.

Knox grinned as he sat down beside the stage. I wondered if he was preparing himself to either catch me or run after me when I bolted from this stupid stage. My eyes shot daggers at Tracey again and all she did was laugh as Archer slid into the booth next to her and whispered something into her ear.

My anger somewhat fizzled out. Was that why she was putting off flirting with Knox? Was it Archer that held her captivated?

The music started up and my heart stopped. Mav started to bob his head to the beat and I could feel my face getting hot already. There weren't very many people in the bar yet but I could feel Rafe's eyes on me as I took a deep breath.

Mav started us off. *"You are my fire,"*

My turn. *"My one desire,"*

I didn't know why I was so afraid. This was my *song* growing up. I had spent countless sleepovers belting this out on the edge of a twin mattress. The few friends I had growing up would blast this while we laid on their carpeted floor and did our nails. It wasn't very many times but the song brought me joy. When it was my turn again, I closed my eyes and leaned forward with the lyrics. I couldn't help myself. The song was a winner. Mav was killing it with backup vocals and when the song came to an end and we were both breathing hard, I couldn't help but grin at him. Maybe this wasn't so bad after all.

Tracey let out a cheer and stood up from the table. It was her turn. She chose *"I Will Survive"* by Gloria Gaynor. She belted out the lyrics like she was getting over a bad breakup. She closed her eyes and put her all into it. Every single emotion. She had me feeling things I wasn't ready to feel. She made me want to dance and she made me want to cry, all at the same time. Knox looked pained from the side of the stage but she wasn't a bad singer. In fact, she was an incredible singer. Her voice was full of soul and it made me envious for a minute. I could listen to her sing all night. Her number ended far too quickly. I cheered with everything in me. I was a proud best friend. But I wasn't disappointed when Mav, Knox, and Gabriel got on the stage.

Tracey grinned from beside me. "This is gonna be good."

"Is this the real life?

Is this just fantasy?

Caught in a landslide

No escape from reality" Gabriel started us off strong with the one song that I knew everyone would all be singing together by the end of it. His voice wrapped around me like a symphony. His brown skin glimmered in the stage lighting and his tight curls on his head bounced as he leaned into the mic. They each took turns singing the long song as Tracey and I belted out the lyrics with them. They each had their arms wrapped around each other as they sang. I couldn't believe how good they were at this. Were all werewolves just naturally good at everything they did? When the guitar solo came around they each played guitar like their lives depended on it. Knox and Mav pressed their backs together as they got down with the music. Sweat was beading on Knox's brow and I was entirely too shocked. He didn't break a sweat when jogging twelve miles, but he was breaking a sweat getting into a fake guitar solo? The men were committed. My cheeks hurt from smiling so hard and by the time the song was over, I had worked up enough courage to look at Rafe.

His yellow eyes were boring into mine. Was there a man behind the wolf? What color eyes did he have when his wolf wasn't at the surface? Was his wolf always at the surface? All these questions were on the tip of my tongue and they were about to spill forward until Knox hopped on stage to do a solo. His eyes left mine and all the wondering in my head went silent.

Why did it matter anyway?

Knox grinned from behind the mic as he pointed to Tracey beside me. She was nursing her third drink and I could smell the wolfsbane on her skin. Her face was composed except for one eyebrow that rose up on her forehead. "This is for you babe!"

She rolled her eyes at that then flipped him off. It only made him smile bigger, which I hadn't thought was possible.

"*Mirror, mirror on the wall*
Don't say it, 'cause I know I'm cute
Louis down to my drawers
LV all on my shoes."

I couldn't help myself. This was a good song. Before I knew it, I was dancing along to Knox's subpar singing and laughing as Tracey twirled me around. She placed her cup on the bar and marched me out to the dance floor. She couldn't help but be pulled in by the beat too. We danced against each other and laughed as the boys whistled across the room. I was going to have permanent wrinkles on my cheeks from this and I didn't mind one bit. Joy overflowed from me as we moved around the dance floor. Yes, the men that had started to flood the bar were hot as sin but it was the last thing I was worried about. For too long I had been worried about the opposite sex. I had chased after it. I had craved it, but tonight I realized that all I needed was me. I could be happy without the bad boy. I could be happy with myself. I didn't need anything else but maybe my best friend and these rowdy Guardians. I didn't need the sex or the alcohol. All I needed was me.

CHAPTER 54
JADE RIVERS

The boys took a break from the karaoke and we all sat at the bar as more people milled in. Tracey pointed out each of the supernatural races while we sat there and she ordered another drink. She pointed to a pale couple in the back. Their eyes flashed red before they blinked back to a dark color. "Those are vampires."

I could have guessed that one. Then there was the group of grunge men and women. They had piercings in their faces and tattoos covering their skin where their leather and fishnets weren't. They had intimidating hair cuts and from what I could see, most of the men wore eyeliner. Tracey held her glass up to one of the girls in greeting and they smiled. Their teeth were sharpened into points. "Those are witches."

I cocked an eyebrow. "They are?"

Tracey shrugged. "Not all supernaturals are the same. There are different kinds of witches. I think those are bone witches. They use bones and hag stones to predict the future, or versions of it."

"What about everyone else?" I whispered before I took a sip of my water.

Tracey leaned back against the bar and rested her elbow on it. "Wolves. Some are rogues, some are from neighboring packs, and the rest are from the Crimson Pack."

"What happened to the lockdown?" I couldn't help but ask. It must have taken a lot to get Rafe to come off of it.

Tracey chewed on her lip as she looked at Rafe over my shoulder. As soon as we had made our way to the bar, he had abandoned his post and went to the other side of the room. He was such a party pooper. "It's still in place. We have a few of the Guardians here and that's the only reason it was permitted. Plus Mav has a soft spot for you and he told Rafe he was going to initiate kidnapping you if he didn't let us go out. We all needed this. *You* especially."

Another good song blasted through the speakers and I found my body moving to the beat. Tracey put her hand in mine and yanked me right back to the dance floor. The lyrics wrapped around me and my body kept to the beat. Growing up, I had always watched the dancers and wished my parents had put me into some kind of class. I had watched countless music videos and YouTube videos to learn as much as I could growing up. I was glad I had because I knew Rafe was watching as I rolled my hips and dropped to the floor. I rolled my neck and threw my hair and when I looked up, he was right there. I swallowed hard but kept to the beat as his hands found my hips and he pulled me to him. I didn't know what had changed. I didn't know what I did to get him on the floor but I wasn't mad about it.

Yes, I was perfectly okay with making myself happy and doing things for myself. But a small thrill still went through me at the spicy scent that washed over me. The scent of whiskey was stronger than usual, but the pine had something else wrapped around it. Something sensual that was fueling me on.

Sweat rolled down the side of my face as I flicked my head back and rolled my body down Rafe's. His fingers trailed up my arm as he kept up to the beat with his dancing against my back. The trail of his fingers up my arm was intoxicating. But there was nothing like the feeling when those fingers ran across my collarbone and up my neck. The callused joints wrapped around my neck and my knees went weak. But it was his breath on my ear that was my undoing.

"I don't know why I'm here, but I couldn't stay away. You make it impossible for me to keep my hands to myself." His voice sounded strained, tortured. When I looked up at him, I could have sworn his eyes were no longer yellow, but instead a light brown. But it could have been a trick of the light when he blinked and they went back to yellow.

I ran my body up against his as I turned in his arms. He bent low and his nose ran up the side of my neck. The motion made me freeze, then it brought back all the painful memories before he forced a change on me. I jerked back and stumbled over my heels. This was silly. How could I have let him get close to me like this again? I couldn't deny that he made me curious and he was hot as sin. But that's what he was, a sin. Something forbidden that was going to get me hurt all over again. He reached toward me but then a body at my back had his hand falling back to his side. I stumbled once again, stupid heels, and the smell of Mav wrapped around me. He smelled like citrus and peppermint. It soothed something inside of me.

His hands wrapped around the top of my shoulders while he guided me back to the bar. Tracey's straw hung from her mouth in shock. "What the hell was that? I mean, it was hot as hell, but like, what happened?" I didn't think I had ever heard her so flustered before.

I shook my head before I looked back at the dance floor over my shoulder. Rafe was gone. "I have no idea." I couldn't have kept the disappointment from my voice even if I tried.

The rest of the night was filled with the laughter I needed to soothe my soul and confusion about what happened with Rafe. Tracey kept me on the dance floor for the rest of the night, dancing away my blues. But it only kept the blues away for so long. I didn't see Rafe again for the rest of the night. Even when we said goodbye to the guys and Tracey handed me her keys, he was still missing. Mav and Knox promised to follow us back to my house, where we would be staying. Tomorrow was Cabin Clean Up day and I was anxious.

Everyone said you could see the cabin from the Manor but I sure as hell couldn't locate it. I was anxious to see where my new home would be. I drummed my fingers on the steering wheel as Tracey hummed.

"Are you excited for tomorrow?" Tracey's head lolled on the headrest. A few of her corkscrew curls had escaped their bun and were spiraling wildly around her face. Her skin glistened in the glow of the streetlights I drove under.

"Yes, though I am a bit nervous. Alice said it was in need of a lot of work."

Tracey winced beside me. "It's pretty bad off, I won't lie to you. The kids dare each other to go in there."

I rolled my eyes. "What are you gonna do? Warn me that it's haunted?"

Tracey snickered. "Definitely not, Granny already ridded it of the spirits."

That didn't make me feel any better. "I hope we have enough cleaning supplies."

Tracey closed her eyes before she yawned. "I doubt we do. We will be making many trips to the hardware store this weekend. You're gonna need paint too, have you picked out a color scheme?"

I shrugged. "I'm thinking black with gold accents."

Tracey cued. "I like the sound of that."

I smiled and was about to reply but I didn't get the chance. Everything seemed to go into slow motion as our car was hit from the side. I barely registered the sound of crunching metal as my head bounced off of the steering wheel. Before my body could register the pain from that, my seat belt was ripped tight across my body as the car flipped once, then twice. I lost count as we went over and over. My head smacked the headrest and my neck burned from the seatbelt as the car came to a jerking halt upside down. My vision was blurry and something was dripping down the side of my face. My limbs were too heavy to reach up to touch it. All I could do was turn my head and try to grab Tracey but no matter how hard I tried, my body wasn't working the way I needed it to.

"Tracey?" My voice sounded foreign and far away.

She was unconscious and blood was flowing from the bottom of her chin. The wolfsbane in her system wasn't going to let her heal quickly either.

What was wrong with me though? Why was everything still so fuzzy and heavy? I pulled at my seat belt as much as I could with my fading strength but it was no use. My head was too fuzzy. I must have gotten a concussion when my head hit the steering wheel the first time.

The sound of crunching glass gave me hope. The Guardians had followed us home. They were here! My tongue felt swollen in my mouth as I tried to yell to them. "In here! We are okay but hurry!"

The door was yanked off of the side of the car and my seatbelt was cut. Before my body could hit the glass, strong arms wrapped around me and pulled me from the wreckage. My head lolled back in relief until I realized the scent wasn't right. Something smelled *wrong*. It was the same wrongness from the rogue in my class just a few days before. I pushed away from the body carrying me and tried to blink my eyes open. What was wrong with me?

"Who are you?" My voice was slurred before I felt a pinch on my backside. I felt the liquid heat in my blood and for a horrifying moment, I thought of the night Rafe had forced me to into this life. But that wasn't what this was and they couldn't turn me again. No, they injected me with a vial of wolfsbane. They drugged me.

"None of your concern, love. We are going to make sure you get taken care of." My ears were still ringing and I could hardly understand what he was saying. By the grace of God, I understood what the others said.

"Are you sure she's the one?" someone else asked.

"You can't smell it? His scent is all over her." another one said.

"Are there any claim marks?" The other guy didn't sound so sure. "There is another girl in the car but she doesn't have claim marks and has lost a lot of blood."

A little bit of fight came back to me at the mention of my friend. But no matter how hard I tried to fight them, my body wouldn't obey. I was a prisoner in my own body. Was this how Carden had felt? So helpless?

"There aren't any claim marks that I can see." One of them muttered as rough fingers grazed the side of my neck. The exact place Rafe had run his nose along. "Maybe we should take the other one too, just to be safe."

"No," Someone else argued. "The other one smells like the Guardian. We have the right one. Leave the car. Let them find the other girl."

The man that was holding me spoke to someone else beside us. The only thing I could make out were the different scents of them. "Yes, you heard me right, we have secured Rafe Crimson's mate."

To be continued...

If you loved this book please leave a review on amazon. If you hated this book, you can leave a review too. Doesn't have to be long or sappy, just something simple. Reviews help authors make a living. Thanks!

ACKNOWLEDGMENTS

During 2020, my life was not what I thought it would be and not because of the pandemic. In fact, as an introverted extrovert, I loved being locked in my house 98% of the time. But in May of 2020, I almost lost my husband. Not to COVID, but to another disease. Another disease that we didn't know he was fighting until it was almost too late. While my husband was bed ridden, I pushed myself farther into my writing to give me an escape from all the pain and torment I was feeling. We still fight a battle with his disease but thankfully, it isn't as bad as before and hopefully, it will never get there again. So because of all of this, I know that I have to thank my husband. For not only fighting the three weeks he should have died, but also for still pushing me and believing in me through that tough time. He never once doubted me or told me to stop pursuing my dreams and honestly, I don't think he ever will. Through this hard time, this book was born. Thank you Brandon for being my fighter. Thank goodness you'll probably never read this because you will hate these words and all the time I put into thanking you. But you deserve all the praise.

Thank you to my wonderful editor that was obsessed with this book from the very beginning. Brittany, thank you for believing in these crazy ideas and even crazier dreams. Thank you for listening to me rant and sending me pics of hot guys when I'm sad. I will never deserve you. Thank you for being the first official member of the Night Shade family.

Thank you to my frannnnnsssss- Tori and Allison. You fuel my bookish characters with so much depth, humor, and wit. There maybe a few of the characters in this book based off of the both of you.

Thank you to my parents that showed me what a truly health family looked like... eventually ;) IYKYK.

Thank you to my readers, I know without a shadow of a doubt that without you and your constant support and reviews, this book wouldn't be what it is today!

Thank you to my betas that got to read this first and praise it! I was feeling so insecure before y'all flooded me with love and encouragement.

ALSO BY A. LONERGAN

Euphoria

Nostalgia

A. Lonergan's life wasn't always a happily ever after, because of this she knows that sometimes the best stories aren't. She knows that sometimes real life comes with grit and darkness, so her stories do too. She loves to read anything and everything she can get her hands on but she has a soft spot for fantasy.

She lives in southern Louisiana where the food is full of comfort, the people like their tea sweet, and the stories are full of soul.

Printed in Great Britain
by Amazon